Wednesday Blues

ANANYA GUHA

First Publication 2023

Cover Design - Bimbisar Das

Published By: Abhra Pal
O Kolkata Publications
Melbourne, Australia

ISBN 978-93-6038-910-9

 Created with Vellum

*Dedicated to my darlings Arjun, Amaira and my
precious family.
My inspirations – my dearest Baba, Buchu and Dida
wherever you are*

Contents

Foreword

My book of short stories is called "Wednesday Blues". It is in the Genre of Short Stories Fiction for Adults/Young Adults. I invite you to enjoy these stories that are written inspired by events during a span of a lifetime - with every character molded beautifully to match the narrative. The book walks you through the upheavals, the normalcy of our existence edging sometimes at dark extremes. The reader gets to see and experience through my characters how an instance in a human's life can change things for the better or worse and how one often chooses to move forward from that defining moment.

Some of it is left to the reader's imagination and some just harbor our inner happiness and pain keeping the reader hooked to the end of every story.

The first story in the narrative called "The Journey" is inspired by my grandmother Nantu's childhood in 1930s' Nepal. The children of an English professor employed by the Nepalese Royal family growing amidst the opulence of their new life contrasting with their humble roots in a village in Bangladesh.

The second story in my book "Deep Blue Sea" talks about how a young Indian woman Misha – a Chef working in Belfast, with a wonderful career given her passion in the restaurant industry is wound steadfast into a torrid love affair with a young and charming Irish gentleman. It almost seems too good to be true although her obsession seems uncanny and realistic at the same time.

"Tubul and Gemmy" is inspired by a childhood account from my father. It is a heartwarming tale of a dog and his young master amidst a major earthquake in the beautiful hill-station of Darjeeling in India. It narrates beautifully how a pet's love remains unblemished and undeterred despite circumstances.

The fourth story in this book "Wednesday Blues" talks about the life of a young adolescent girl Anoushka and her first crush on a boy in her tutor's class and how she, influenced as a hopeless romantic through novels and movies, finds herself struggling between the perception of love and reality.

"The Rose" is a beautiful account of a four-year-old girl growing up in a well-to-do home in the Industrial city of Damanjodi in India and her perspective on meeting a handicapped child laborer, how they bond and play as one and yet their lives are so different.

"The Masterpiece" tells the story of how a young teenage Indian American girl in Baltimore from a middle-class immigrant home pays the price of empathy she has for a teacher suffering from Parkinson's disease.

"Sundari's Family" is the story of two siblings Buchu and Duggu in Kolkata, India, and their neighborhood pets – Sundari the glorious cat and her exuberant litter of beautiful and energetic kittens.

The last story "Curry Corner" talks of rediscovering

one's existence after a hasty Indian arranged love marriage, a modern twist added to the age-old tradition. The story talks about the aftermath of such a wedding and the effect it has on a young woman Raina's life, hope, career, and dreams.

Hope you savor this incredible journey as I did, drafting these stories across a couple of decades and sometimes with big breaks in between. This book is a small collection in these times of rushed readers and reading. Enjoy!

Ananya

The Journey

The sun was rising in the east, the sky was ochre at the center, silvered at the rims and leaden at the edges. The pines canvassed grotesque shadows on the earth beneath, gyrating wildly in the wind that tore the buds off the rhododendrons. Several yards below lay the diminutive platform, the narrow meter-gauge tracks having long disappeared into oblivion, and the railway station a pitiable structure of wood battering against the winds and gales of the Himalayas.

A *palki*[1] made its way up the rugged terrain, through a craggy mountain path that had been tread upon for centuries, and often had the unpleasant reputation of being visited over by wild herds of elephants. In the dense forest all that could be heard was the *hoon hoona re hoon hoona*, a hoarse cry from the *palkiwalas*[2]. The wind would have chilled any of these able-bodied men to their bones as they staggered on bare bodied and bare footed, but for the cry that seemed to have a soothing effect on their constitution. The *palki* stalled when it reached the peak. A white streak of foam gurgled down, trickling amidst the boulders, and caressing the gravel below. The *palki* or the *tamjam* as it was locally known in Nepali, was lowered and the four men untwined their *gamchas*[3] from their heads and moistened them in the sparkling waters. They pressed the cloth on their knees and arms, cupping and drinking the water from the stream to their soul's content. The sun peeped from behind a snowy peak that had assumed a bronze sheen as if polished very recently under the eager eye of an artisan.

There they ran free, the *palkiwalas,* not at the slow pace with which they had ascended. The wild terrain was at their disposal, and they knew it only too well. There were raised voices, the topic of concern being the presence of a *khet*[4] nearby and the fortunate absence of its owner. They wanted to make the most of it. Radishes and onions were torn off the ground with unmatched dexterity, deskinned with long nails, washed in the stream, for they had a penchant for cleanliness, and consumed raw, chewing consciously or unconsciously away to nourish their tired bodies. It was the autumn of 1933, the trees on the peaks were evergreen unlike their deciduous colleagues in the valleys below. Those trees shone a coppery hue from afar, the nearest being a *Krishnachura* tree several feet beneath on the eastern slope that lay ahead.

I then at my eleventh year of existence and my younger brother Khoka, a trifle four years younger to me and under my special care, as we made our way to our lodgings in Kathmandu, Nepal. My father was a professor of English, a double M.A. during his times who taught the Nepalese *Maharaja's* sons. We thus spent most of our childhood in Nepal. On this occasion, we were returning from Dhaka, Pirpur in Bangladesh after the *Durga Pujo* at *didima's*[5] place. Stacked along with our miniature forms were bottles of *mishti aamer achaar*[6], *aamshotto*[7], homemade guava jam, *taler gur*[8], *shutki maach*[9] and the likes destined to last an entire year. In Nepal such luxuries were atypical, if not unheard of. We were the only Bengali residents of the area.

Ma could not accompany us when we left Pirpur three days ago and it was father's Gorkha *durwaan*[10] who had monitored our journey right from our village in Bangladesh to the only railway station in the area, Amlekganj Nepal. Mother had acquired a mild fever when we left and the village *baddi*[11] diagnosed her with the ague. She would soon follow suit, I thought and so would those lovely mornings when Ma, Khoka and I would get up early and pick roses and marigolds from the *Rani's*[12] garden for our morning prayers. We were fortunate to enjoy this special luxury as father was a respected name, and everybody including the *maali*[13] knew that he was close to the *Raja*[14].

The Nepali New Year was but a few days away, I thought musingly. It was one of those rare occasions when we were given an opportunity to see the royals in person and seek their blessings. I remembered each time, I used to gasp when I beheld the monarchs in their flowing silk garbs. The *Maharaja*[14], his crown studded with innumerable diamonds would smile down upon you, the *Rani* in her elaborate diamond and ruby tiara, elegant necklaces in pearl with gold lattice-work, her feet adorned with beautiful golden anklets, would say *tipo tipo* aka pick it up, when you saluted her with a coin.

One may have easily been blinded as the lights in the palace would cause the diamonds to sparkle beyond measure, another reason why we had never seen the monarchs' faces quite clearly. Then there would be the *Raja's* banquet, the exquisite food that would be served in grand silverware.

I specially admired those tiny silver *koutos*[15] that would be given to us at the end of the grand feast containing myriad spices, raisins large and small in varying hues, cashews, cardamoms raw and ripe, cloves that smelt heavenly and lord knows what else. In the *kouto's* tiny shelves which you could pull out each time, there were rare treats for us children like when you wanted to taste the sweet juice of raw cardamom or savor the experience of putting a large brown raisin inside your mouth.

One of these days we would visit the *Neelkantha* shrine in the king's *phiton*[16].

Ma would often take us there since the time *Didi*[17] had left us for a couple of years to study in Calcutta. It was Ma's coping mechanism to deal with the times she sorely missed seeing her firstborn. Khoka and I simply adored the massive statue of *Vishnu*[18] in black granite reclining on a pool of clear water and loved playing in the premises of the massive temple.

I woke up as if from a daze, when our *palki* pulled up outside our home. The shrill cry of a woman's wail seemed to wrench at my heart and seemed vaguely familiar. My knees trembled when I descended with my brother holding on to the loose end of my small saree.

As we entered, I saw my father lying almost lifeless on the bamboo mat where *Ma* combed and tied my hair each evening. "Nantu! The cholera has taken your Ma forever away from us in Bangladesh" shrieked our housekeeper sobbing.

They had just got the telegram and as these words pervaded my system, I saw my father slowly get up, his eyes blinded with tears, his arms outstretched, and we ran for respite to his bosom.

———

1 palanquin
    2 palanquin bearers
    3 turbans
    4 farmland
    5 grandmother
    6 sweet mango pickles
    7 mango fruit bark
    8 palm jaggery cakes
    9 dried cured fish
    10 security guard
    11 physician/doctor
    12 queen
    13 gardener/landscaper
    14 king
    15 small jewelry box
    16 horse carriage
    17 elder sister
    18 Indian Deity Vishnu

———

Deep Blue Sea

Deep blue sea and the sky above, none could catch her eye. The colossal waves seemed to surrender into nothingness as they gurgled on the small white pebbles strewn on the otherwise sandy beach. The smaller waves were destined to a similar fate as if they knew their efforts, albeit relentless, would go in vain.

To an outsider, the mood was strangely somber or probably a concoction of depression and sagging anticipation. The sea blue cupid wallpaper and the half-drawn satin cream curtains did nothing to camouflage her pain as she gazed listlessly across the glass barrier that separated her and the waves. As she desperately clinched on to her beliefs and fought off her worst nightmares, she knew the conflict within her was rising to cataclysmic proportions. She knew her feelings wouldn't ebb like the tide. It was already too late. Biting sarcasm, a stinging taunt, an acidic reaction? What caused it? She anxiously sought an explanation. Was it the color of her skin?

Shuddering at the thought, she rose from the

exquisite teak and mahogany dining table and slumped into an armchair. Jet black hair framed most of her face as she silently closed her tired red eyes and seemingly indulged into a distant reverie.

She had not yet accustomed herself to the winds and gales of the region as she fought her way out of her tiny silver Smart twin-seater and walked down a gentle, lush green slope that led to a breath-taking view of the Atlantic. She was almost submissive as the wind tugged heavily at her thin white crepe shirt, almost threatening to pull it away. 'No one's watching,' she promptly assured herself as she crossed her arms around her chest, trying to hold back the raging wind.

A rugged cliff wall of contrasting black basalt and brown earth stood out in the distance. Her awe was intangible as she saw below a vast sheath of blue and marine green ecstasy dotted with countless rocks braving the sparkling waters. Never had she seen a sight so utterly captivating in its entirety.

A few miles ahead stood a crescent of white chalk in the shape of a castle emerging amidst the ocean, whiter still with the countless seagulls resting on its rugged lime fortresses. To her sides stretched the meandering Irish coastal route, a greyish blue ribbon lining the coast, known to kiss the nine Glens of Antrim, the seat of Irish folklore and history. She read from the tour booklet about the unfriendly Irish fairies, the leprechauns. These two-foot tall, cranky, gruff men clad in a green coat, hat, and a shoemaker's apron prefer to pass their time making shoes for other fairies and are trusted to guard fairy treasures in pots of gold very carefully. Rainbows and the sound of a shoemaker's hammer provide humans with visual and audio cues as to a leprechaun's whereabouts and hidden treasure.

Misha let out a sigh, gulping in mouthfuls of the

cool salt breeze. The money she had saved aside for hiring a car that weekend had indeed not gone in vain; for all she knew, there was still more to see. Even the heavens above were on her side. It was a dazzling blue morning in July, and a lovely rainbow was taking shape just ahead. A leprechaun's sure to be around, she mused.

She took a small leap and found herself sitting cross-legged a few meters away from the cliff's edge. Sitting cross-legged in one jump was a trick she had perfected since childhood. She closed her eyes in reminiscence of how she and her baby sister often used to compete on who did it the fastest. She mused on how wonderful it would be to have her sister there at that very instant. She was missing her family dearly.

Driving along next, she came across the spectacular ruins of the Dunluce castle perched on a cape or rocks on the way to her next destination, the world-famous Carrick-A-Rede rope bridge. 'Marvelous!' she bellowed, driving past the castle. She was in despair now for not yet being the proud owner of a digital camera and only had circumstances to blame. She knew only too well that her little bearings would not let her afford such luxury just yet. 'Dad's good old Canon analog would do just fine,' she said to herself, pepping up at the sheer thought and stopping her car inadvertently to capture some precious moments. 'Just 12 more to go,' she cogitated, thinking how best to use the remaining piece of reel to her nonpareil advantage.

Pulling up at the driveway a few minutes from the Carrick-A-Rede rope bridge, she dismantled her lunch from the knapsack in the boot of her car, a sumptuous Indian paratha roll secured in foil with lamb kebab, green chutney, and pickled onions. Famished since morning and yet with an unbridled desire to relish the fantasies of this unknown and magical place, the hunger soon left her, and she callously stuffed it into the folds of her oversized white bag. The bag was like a second skin to her in this distant land, where she carried her Indian passport, visa papers, and family pictures.

Her soul yearned for adventure. But, from hearsay, the place she was visiting was 'not for the faint-hearted'. Not that she cared, but deep inside, a child within her protested in the most vociferous way possible. She heard it, too but preferred to submerge it within her newfound excitement. It was a straight twenty-minute walk to the rope bridge, which lay at the foot of a hundred and forty steps that led to the fishermen's chasm. She trudged along the undulating track, which practically traversed an array of cliff tops. Watching each cliff caressed on its sides by the divinely blue and turquoise ocean, Misha quietly hummed 'Climb Every Mountain' from The Sound of Music. 'Well, if there is paradise somewhere, this would be it,' she thought. Having grown up watching the Sound of Music, she remembered each of those Sunday afternoons that were spent watching the film over and over with all the kids from the neighborhood. She would identify with Mary, the most silent of Captain von Trapp's children in the movie. She would remember how her mother would fry onions in gram flour batter and serve them with a sweet chutney on Sunday evenings for her friends. On lone Saturday evenings, when she would snack on onion rings at home, she would think of Ma's unbridled affection, her amazing cooking, and the comfort of her own home back in India.

But Misha was living her dream in this foreign land,

and everything exquisite seemed to converge surprisingly at that very moment. No sooner had she reached the narrow flight of steps that led to the swaying bridge separating the 24-meter chasm over a portion of sea dotted with boulders, the child inside her gasped in horror. A long-forgotten fear of heights stared nastily at her face. She felt the earth slip beneath her feet as she cautiously disembarked the last flight of stairs that led to the swinging rope bridge.

Revulsion and excitement engaged her otherwise calm self and fought mightily for prominence. She could gauge everyone's enthusiasm behind her from the commotion that reached her. Still surprised that she had managed to decipher bits and pieces of what they were saying, considering how scared she was.

Of one thing, she was certain. None of them were as petrified or as much in a dilemma as she was. There were two ways to go from here, and she knew her return would be an act too cowardly amidst all the frenzy that surrounded her. She admonished the cry of terror that rose from her soul, the same feeling that seemed to redden her ear lobes and flush her cheeks. A vague emotion egged her on.

Her first step on the rack of wood held fast by a herculean piece of rope supporting her beneath and, on the sides, added strength to her terrified soul. A few more steps and she soon found herself at the center of the object of her trepidation. "I half conquered the monster," she thought as she sought to explain who the monster was, her conscience or the length of rope that held her weight and swayed to and fro in perfect harmony.

She opened her eyes wide for the first time, and her gaze soon wandered to where it was destined to reach. As she peered through the piers of teak below, she saw several feet underneath, a green-blue foam chained sea, lash mercilessly against the defenseless mounds of black basalt. The waves unsatiated struck each time with renewed vigor - leaving behind a trail of unrestrained froth. The gulls whining peevishly, apparently lamenting the game of torment below, flew in circles above.

Muffled voices roused her from that state of stupor. The bridge had started gyrating at an urgent pace thanks to the antics of a troupe of children who had just stepped in. Misha catapulted into a dizzying mangle of light and sound as the world slowly receded into oblivion and a tunnel of darkness gradually approached her. Her knees, sapped of the last vestige of strength at the ensuing terror, gave way, and she plunged headlong into the threaded pier.

A yelp of remorse was all she heard, and then a warm, long, sinewy hand grasping her firmly by the waist lifted her off her falling feet with remarkable alacrity. Her eyes saw nothing apart from the maze, which still blinded her. The lone sinewy hand, promptly followed by another, held her unflinchingly now. Misha continued to perceive the gently rocking bridge below quaintly, but the sensation did not last long as she soon found herself rested on a bench atop firm soil.

'Are you okay?'

The first few words were music to her ears. Indeed, she had lived to see the rest of her life. The very thought resurrected her from her state of trance. Misha opened her eyes to meet the angel who had brought on this divine intervention. What else could it have been?

He indeed was an apparition - auburn hair, clear blue eyes set close, piercing yet gentle, offsetting caramel brown eyebrows bridged by a high bronzed nose and defined cheekbones. His face was lightly freckled yet masculine with an immaculate jaw line and a generous mouth that she saw curve ever-so slightly out of genuine concern. In short, breathtakingly handsome, he was an Adonis, and the placid air about him only accentuated his features.

He was kneeling right before her in his faded blue denim and short-sleeved grey linen shirt, which concealed a fantastic physique as Misha noted sheepishly for the first time. She was still speechless. She had been confident of so many things she had to tell this messenger of God, but the circumstances had kept her tongue-tied. She was not even sure which gesture could suffice to thank him.

"Do you need a hand? Or maybe some water?" he said, motioning for a bottle to a colorfully clad woman standing not far behind him. His accent suggested he was Irish.

"Yes, I'd like some water," said Misha fidgeting about her disheveled self and finally finding her voice. After a few gulps down, she was calmer, and her body slowly recuperated its strength.

She was on her feet now. He stood up on seeing her. At just over six feet, he was a strapping Irish male with reddish blonde hair probably in his late twenties.

"I don't know how to thank you!" she blurted out.

"Wait, wait…don't be in such a hurry," he quirked. "You still have to make your way back," he said, flashing the most brilliant smile.

Misha smiled responsively but was too shy to let her embarrassment show. Instead, she now observed that they were on the other side and almost let out an involuntary sigh when the prospect of making her way back promptly dawned on her.

"Wasn't I a Samson?" he commented with a lopsided

grin lightening the ambience as he sensed her discomfort.

Misha quickly recovered. "Yes!" she answered gleefully. "You were a hero!"

"Hello, I am Misha," she said and lunged her hand forward.

He shook it warmly. "I am Roger, your savior," he bespoke with a good-natured smile. Misha suppressed a grin.

Soon after, Roger introduced her to his friend Stella, a petite Irish brunette with small smiling eyes peeking from behind her dark brown bangs. She was clad in a flower-patterned summery green dress and wore the most extraordinary cross of diamonds across her bare neck.

"Why don't you join us while we are here?"

Misha was in the mood to politely decline the offer, but something told her otherwise. She ruminated quietly for a few minutes before asking if they were sure, it wouldn't be a problem for them both.

"Hey, it's not like we are out on a date or something. Stella is my colleague!"

"So don't even bother intruding on us," added Stella showcasing a set of pearly white teeth and shoving Roger away playfully.

They all laughed in unison. Soon they had arrived at the edge of the fisherman's pier, another cliff that plunged brazenly into the sea.

"Mademoiselle, if you would be so kind enough to offer me your hand?" interrupted Roger as they ventured to crane their necks perilously over the ledge to better view the most overwhelming scenery. "I wouldn't want to let you have your way for a close second time this afternoon," he thundered, pouting his chest, and going down to his knees to hold out his hand.

The ladies ended up laughing uncontrollably at the sudden gesture.

She had fallen in love with his hands as they held her in seize. She enjoyed the lug, the restraint, the reflexive squeeze, the mastery in those enormous hands, and for a moment, her brain was benumbed in a vague perception of eternal happiness.

As they doubled back to return to the parking lot, it was only natural that Roger would maneuver her journey across the rope bridge. First, he coiled an arm around her waist, clipping her left hand on his one side while he asked her to abide by the bridge railing using her right. Then, nudging her tenderly at her visible alarm, delicate words of encouragement whispered into her right ear, he managed to get her across without much ado.

During their chat, she came to know that he was a resident of Northern Ireland. Although he mainly worked in Cyprus, he was stationed in Belfast for two months, contracting for a third party. Once his project was over, he would head back to Limassol in Cyprus. Stella worked for the organization that had hired Roger's services and they were collaborating on the same project. Misha, in equal breath, introduced herself as a chef working for 'The Copper Wok, ' a popular Indian food joint in Belfast.

"I adore Indian food!" boomed Roger as they entered their respective cars. "Especially Dosa ..." he said, puckering his lips as if in ecstasy. "Maybe we'll see each other soon, and next time, I might just take some recipes from you."

They drove off with the customary pleasantries and goodbyes.

Misha rounded off the day with a visit to the Giants Causeway, the seat of the Spanish Armada shipwrecks. A battalion of volcanic rocks in the shape of hexagons strewn into the sea reminded her of the mystic stone path that led from the southernmost tip of the Indian peninsula to the sheltered quays of Sri Lanka - the land bridge created by the *hanuman*[1] army and associated with the Indian epic Ramayana. There was a myth here, too, that bespoke of an Irish giant named Finn McCool who would use the Causeway to walk to Scotland to fight his Scottish nemesis, Benandonner.

Monumental peaks leaning precariously over the ravaging sea harnessing a bed of well-beaten tracks which shepherds and tourists had trodden for ages conspired to create the most mesmerizing vision, and she soaked in the beauty of it all.

It was the month of August, and the rains seemed to pour incessantly as Misha rustled up a chicken hariyali, a dish comprised of succulent pieces of chicken in creamy spinach gravy. The aroma wafted across the glass and wooden door, which opened and closed in intervals as the waiters and waitresses bustled carrying trays of aesthetically decorated authentic Indian food.

Misha was the primary assistant to the head chef, the overpowering and garrulous Ranaut, all of sixty, pot-bellied, his trademark salt and pepper mustache twisted at the ends, the mark of a true *khandani bawarchi*[2] and laughter lines that speckled his mouth, eyes and creased his forehead into innumerable folds. Old Ranaut was good to his junior chefs if they did not care to challenge his mastery in the kitchen.

However, he took to the it differently, in the way that Misha chose to persuade him. She would work extra hours and buy the ingredients out of her own purse to convince Ranaut of new dishes, recipes, and innovations in the kitchen. It was a slower process, but she could always convince him in the end. So, it wasn't surprising that Misha's growth as a chef in the closed quarters of 'The Copper Wok' had been more than substantial in the last fifteen months of her stay.

She had already been promoted twice from Trainee chef to the Secondary assistant and subsequently to her current position as deputy Sous Chef. Her pay, too, had matured from a measly sum of eight hundred pounds to a respectable twelve hundred.

It had been an unusually long Saturday which meant brisk business and almost double the average amount of work for the chefs. It was half past ten in the night, and everyone was getting ready to bring the shutters down at eleven.

She poured the contents of the heavy-bottomed wok, a steaming mixture of flavorful succulent chicken and creamed spinach, into a copper bowl - the shape of an ancient oil lamp and topped it with a dollop of cream. Some piping hot naans from the tandoor smelling divinely of freshly baked bread and molten butter and a sprig of mint leaves in a small pool of slightly sweetened and spiced yogurt were the accompaniments that concluded her last dish for the evening.

In the lone recluse of a dimly lit quadrant at 'The Copper Wok', a guest, almost unintelligible, waited in suppressed anticipation. His enthusiasm was palpable when his senses overtook his senses as the dish of his choice was served sizzling on the table. Strangely enough, it seemed to overpower him thinly in its superb aroma as he instantly remarked, "Incredible!" almost belligerently.

'The Copper Wok' was unarguably one of the best in the business. Located in the most profitable quarter of south Belfast, a nerve center in the otherwise sleepy metropolis after dark, it almost always did brisk business. Ranaut's uncle, a Sikh Chef, had laid the first foundations of one of the oldest Indian eateries in Belfast, having bought that piece of property right off a Catholic Cloth merchant on Dublin Road several years ago. A meager capital, a staggering wooden shack as his facility, and him and his wife as the only cooks in the humble establishment had totaled his paltry possessions then.

A sprawling restaurant, expert chefs scurrying about the kitchen uncovering extraordinary delicacies and serving curries in traditional brass vessels, servers skilled on the job, proficient lounge managers, and a décor that would even put the embellishments at a star's home in Bollywood to shame would be how one would choose to describe 'The Copper Wok' today. With it came a generous dosage of the ethnology associated with the great Indian hospitality psyche. A visit to the restaurant would entail; first, a cool mist of rosewater caressing one's face, then one would find themselves seated on a plush velvet sofa ornate with golden tassels surrounded in finery, exquisite paintings, silken tapestry, et al. The guest could choose from a wide selection of items on the menu or elect preferences or specialties from individual chefs.

Having indulged entirely in the most delectable of meals, the guest now rose to summon a server.

"Would you call the chef for me, please? I wish to congratulate and thank them in person," he professed.

Misha soon appeared, led by the Lounge Manager himself. He saw her taking off her chef's cap and fluffing her hair lightly as she left the confines of the kitchen. Her black hair fell in easy ripples on her white chef's garb, and the flush from the heat in the kitchen turning a pale orange on her bronze skin leisurely rose to her translucent cheeks. The whites in her doe eyes were mildly pink from the day's exhaustion, while her thawing languid gaze wandered searchingly, as she silently approached him. She looked tired yet beautiful in an exhausted sensuous way.

He stood up when they were a few meters away and smiled the most hypnotic and disarming of smiles. No sooner were they within hearing distance of each other than he proclaimed.

"Madam, I am honored to be here, and honestly, this is the best Chicken Hariyali I have ever tasted. Incidentally, I also happen to be a stickler for Indian cuisine. That obviously means my opinion could be trusted!"

They were now facing each other.

"Have we met before?" he concluded questioningly; the smile now wider as his gaze wandered to her slightly parted lips as they trembled before she spoke.

"Roger! I don't believe this"

"Oh gosh, so excited to see you here! Did you plan this?"

"That's your last guess for today," he said, giving a rather affectionate smirk.

"Well, honestly, I had come to check if you had fibbed about being a chef in the first place."

"Roger!" bellowed Misha laughing as they both hugged each other.

She offered to join him after a quick change and did. The Copper Wok was bringing down its shutters for the evening when they walked out in the calm and clear summer night.

"I generally take a cab when it's late, especially on Saturdays. Too many kids are out on the street partying away, and sometimes getting carried away isn't that difficult.

"I might land up beer brained," commented Misha as they crossed a group of teenagers just across the road, as they punched each other in turns tossing around beer bottles and soda cans.

"You have me to walk you today," he suggested majestically and flexing in a jovial sort of way.

"Though the only thing I crave is a six-pack. I used to have it eons ago. Somehow it just evades me these days. Maybe I am really getting old!" he bludgeoned out, visibly sad at his obvious misfortune. He looked affectionately at Misha as he spoke. She followed his gaze gently careen her curves and the orange chiffon dress that perfectly silhouetted her. Her bronze skin shone warm under the streetlights, her eyes still mildly red from the day's exhaustion. She was very attracted to Roger in that very moment. She also found it funny that she still was in love with his hands. A six-pack didn't really matter!

A symposium on ages, birthdays, and sun signs followed and culminated with an invitation to her apartment the following Sunday - the only day she was off from work. He hugged her a warm goodbye at the gate, a quick peck and Misha walking into the living room happily convinced that she had not smelt of ginger and garlic.

The first three days of the week passed by in an instant. On the fourth day he sent her a text saying he was watching 'If Only', his favorite movie, and was making a valiant attempt at trying *rajma*[3] curry for dinner that evening. She gave him some quick pointers on how to cook these in as many lines as two text messages could offer. He got back, saying he had already looked these up on the internet.

"How foolish of me," she reasoned. "Should have guessed that!"

The next few days were unbearably long as Misha struggled to decide on a menu for their lunch date.

On Saturday evening, as Misha kneaded sweet flour and desiccated milk into a soft dough for Gulab Jamuns the next day, she got another text confirming that he would be in by eleven the following morning.

The text only multiplied her woes. She rattled, standing alone in the kitchen, knowing fully well that she was not even done with half her cooking, and it was already ten at night. She had taken the evening off, especially for this, and that, too, fell short.

She thought first of requesting him to delay his visit for a few hours, citing what she thought would be justified under the circumstances - she hadn't had the time to cook and would prefer if he showed up a little later. She mulled over the consequences and again thought otherwise. After all, she was still not sure if her request could be taken negatively or worse still be considered too rude. It certainly would in India. It would be unkindly even to suggest such a thing to a guest, let alone implement it back home.

The phone sang to a tone of Elvis's Wooden Heart the following morning when Misha was still in the bathtub. Washing off the last remnants of shampoo from her hair she ran off, wrapping a towel around her. Roger was just round the corner by the next street and was having trouble recognizing her home.

She offered to be at the door as soon as she could. The directions she had given were too complicated for comprehension in her head, but then she had never been good at that sort of thing.

A Magenta boat-necked top accentuating her long neck and a pair of navy-blue jeans ridden on in haste, a hint of lip gloss and a smear of kohl from the night before smudging under her wet lashes, hair still dripping and plastering her top smugly across her back, an oversized pair of feathery red bedroom slippers and Misha was at the door. She wondered if she had ever looked worse.

If only I had been Irish, she thought, I would have comfortably culminated my culinary histrionics eons ago. Steak and potatoes or even fried fish were so much easier to prepare. Indian food always takes forever without help like she did get at the restaurant and clearly broke her back this morning. If only I had all the time in the world to be ready for this dapper date! 'If Only' she thought and smiled, reminiscing the movie she had recently made a point to see after she knew it was his favorite.

A gleaming Porsche convertible in Pristine silver pulled up at the gate and she instantly recognized the handsome man at the wheel. She waved back merrily as he parked his magnificent vehicle across the neighbor's driveway. Within seconds he stepped out, smiling in a shirt hued pure icy blue, sleeves rolled comfortably halfway, a pair of well-fitted grey jeans, and carrying a gorgeous bouquet of brilliant pink and white orchids for the lady. She was thrilled as she ushered him in, mumbling about not possessing a vase. 'I don't have a vase at home either,' he instantly announced.

Lunch was eaten in silence a scrumptious spread of crisp home-made butter naans, fragrant pilaf made with basmati rice, shahi paneer and lamb korma. Rounding off the meal with a couple of warm syrupy Gulab Jamuns served with scoops of vanilla ice cream seemed just perfect. A volley of praises from Roger followed as Misha beamed inwardly at her prowess. Did someone say the only way to a man's heart is through his stomach?

"Would you like to go on a drive?" he asked as soon as they finished their meal.

Ecstatic as she was, she offered to join him in a minute. A quick brush through her hair, a dab of her favorite perfume and she was set to roll. They drove down the quay to Hollywood in East Belfast.

"This is my parents' place," quipped Roger as they sped past a terracotta red brick villa amidst a garden with roses of varying color and decree. Potted plants, some of them in full bloom, hung in neat rows from the balcony and added that extra hint of fantasy to the fairy house.

"Could you bring the hood down for a minute? I'd really love that!" Misha pleaded, hardly able to suppress her excitement.

And down it came, catapulting her into the most unblemished and cheerful moment of her entire living existence till then. The silver convertible rode power-fully on the highway, now fully radiant in the August sunshine. The wind exploded in wholesome propor-tions wreaking havoc on her tousled hair. Their eyes met, and Misha instantly fathomed the gaze.

Six months down, she was at his place spending the evening like she did often. He had cooked up a decent meal of cheese ravioli, a bulgar spring onion salad, and an orange cheesecake for dessert.

"This is the first time; I've cooked for a date!" he proclaimed. She curled up against him on the sofa as she ate pausing occasionally to entwine her body in his enormous arms and his incessant kisses. Her insides churned in unrepressed passion.

"I don't get married before I'm 40," pronounced Roger pulling back a morsel of cheese ravioli that clung to the corner of his lips.

"You are kidding me, right?" asked Misha, unperturbed.

"It's just been six months! So why are we even discussing this?" he suggested.

"I don't understand!" said Misha. "It's not like we are getting married right away! Do we even know where this is heading? Aren't we in a relationship and expecting the best to happen? No one has seen tomorrow, but it is today that we could consider making better!" she asserted, sipping from a pint of Baileys Irish cream he had served that evening and breaking off into a good-natured grin. The whiskey had disengaged her as she made a pout with the last remnants of the lingering sweet drink inside her mouth and locked her lips against his. This alone she knew was paradise.

He dropped her home that night and they kissed in the car before they parted. They would meet again in three weeks. Roger was flying the day after to Dublin, where his ailing grandmother stayed at a Senior Home. He would be there for a week, meeting her and other close friends, and then fly directly to Cyprus for work.

"I am at this wedding here in Dublin and they are trying to set me up with this silly brunette. Help me Misha" he messaged one evening. A slight pang of jealousy struck her soul, but she buried it instantly and replied that she wished she was there to watch the fun. She was out shopping and had mainly picked up an exquisite white and blue Chinese porcelain flower vase from Debenhams, a vase that a certain Mr. Roger at 86 Grinhark Road needed. She had made grand plans for his birthday and subsequently found herself smiling stupidly at a mirror in the mall, lost in the wilderness of her own imagination.

She waited for the day he would return. He messaged

her when he landed at the George Best Airport. Come online at eleven, he told her. Misha hurried back from work, and they chatted till late in the night. "I missed you," he told her. I love the way you massage my back." Misha could not sleep that night as she lay in bed thinking about the wonderful times they had spent. It was time she told her sister about her boyfriend.

A week later, they met for lunch. It was a Friday and his birthday. They met outside his office in Lanyon Place. Misha handed Roger the gift and his birthday card that she had lovingly sown for him out of colorful pieces of fabric.

"I guess you better hurry," he told her as he handed her a box of sweets in return. He had got them from Cyprus. "My work mates could be here any moment, and they would ask me a dozen questions" he told her. Misha complied. Her contentment on seeing him had surpassed all boundaries, and she was thrilled at the box of colorful sweets on a hand-painted Cypriot tray. Her grand plans for the day were not precisely under-way, but she was cheerful regardless.

That evening she received a text message saying – Things can never work out between us. I am four years older than you and hence need to be sensible. Please understand.

Misha's head throbbed in agitation. She tried reasoning if the circumstances could equate to a prac-tical joke executed in full grandeur. She assured herself it could only be a full-blown excuse to meet that evening.

She took a cab to his place and rang the bell. He opened, bleary-eyed and dressed in a worn brown tee. He grimaced on seeing her. Misha's eyes gleamed in anticipation and fear as he hesitatingly led her inside.

"This is not going to happen. Nothing can come out

of this!" he imparted as he motioned her to sit on the sofa.

"What's wrong with you?" she asked.

"It's time I spoke sensibly," he blazoned out.

"But we'll work something out. Where's the problem? I'll get a permanent job here. I'll tell my parents. We can get married when we are ready."

"I don't want to get married. I may not get married at all or wait till I'm 40. What will you do here until then? Also, it's just been a few months. We don't even know if this is leading somewhere, and I can't ask you to change the course of your life for me."

"This is insane," she retaliated, stomping around in disbelief.

"Can I call you a cab?" he proclaimed finally.

"Did I hear you right?"

"You did! I want you to leave".

"Okay! So that's what I am worth to you? You won't even hear me out. I am not dying to marry you in case you think I am. You are completely ruthless and disgusting!" she suggested flaring out completely.

"You don't get to abuse me standing right here in front of me and inside my house."

The cab had arrived. Roger held the door out for her and kept mum until her taxi sped off. After a sleepless night, and a flurry of unanswered text messages to his phone, Misha went to work on Saturday bleary-eyed and visibly drained of any iota of strength whatsoever. She had somehow convinced herself of being too harsh on Roger the night before.

Ranaut let her off for the rest of the weekend, suspecting a bad illness as she passed out twice in the restaurant, recuperating each time to the aroma of lime on ice and soda offered by her distraught colleagues.

She took a cab from the restaurant that evening,

asking the cabbie to drive over to the street in Hollywood where Roger lived. As they pulled up at house number 86, she walked up firmly to the door and knocked. No one responded. A small, printed note partially scribbled in neat handwriting was on the door latch.

"Shifted base to Cyprus. Can be contacted at my apartment in Limassol."

A phone number and address were printed underneath in bold.

She only had to follow her conscience, but a million voices pleaded with his innocence and animosity in equal breath. She pined for the call that would pacify her pain that night, but her pleas ended only in failure. The next morning, she booked a flight to Limassol for the following day, indubitably putting all her self-honor at stake.

The city was a scorching 38 degree centigrade compared to the measly fifteen-degree summer in Northern Ireland, not that it mattered as she was used to warmer temperatures in India. She arrived at the apartment a few meters off an abandoned extension on the Avmidou beach only to find it open. She had been waiting for nearly three hours till then in imperforate silence marred occasionally by her crying, tears wetting the pristine white armchair until the door hinge creaked before being flung open.

In walked an Aphrodite, a woman of exceptional beauty, shiny golden tresses framing her petite face and rippling in clusters below to loosely caress her nymph's bottom. She was wearing a white and gold bikini with specks of sand dotting her alabaster skin in places and caking a pair of dainty bare feet. Trailing her was a very handsome man in a bathing suit, wearing a smile impeccably disarming.

The scorching mid-afternoon Cypriot sun peeped in through the door and seemed to faintly brighten that forlorn moment.

---

1 Indian monkey god Hanuman
　　2 royal cook
　　3 red beans

Tubul and Gemmy

It was Tubul's third year at his school in Darjeeling. Having just returned from Kolkata after the *Pujo*[1] he was all ready for the new term, braced to face the coveted oddities and joys that this year would offer him. Especially since from this day on, in history, he would have the privilege of finally going to an only boys' school, now that his primary school years were complete. This would essentially mean a rare treat in the form of not having to share or, at times, forgo priceless treasures in the likeness of marbles, warty toads, sparrows with broken wings, multicolored pebbles from the hill streams, and even coca cola bottle caps at the hands of none other than the tantrum-throwing, demanding, almost always tearful female species without ever giving up a fight. He had uncovered this rare gospel about women at an early stage of his existence or so he thought.

He closed his eyes in silent anticipation of the events that would follow and almost sniffed in relief as he stepped into the premises of his new school. No longer would he be ridiculed by Bumba and Khokon, his elder brothers, for being spotted in shorts and accompanying Baccha and Shankari, his neighbors - the little girls who escorted him to Maharani Girls School for his primary years.

The first day at the boy's school had been genuinely convivial in every sense of the word with Shibu, Jolly, Bhendu, the twins Bulu – Bomphat for company, all Tubul's playmates from the *para*[2]. The day was spent gamboling the grounds at Darjeeling Boys Government High School, exploring every nook and cranny that evoked anything bordering on enigma. The school building was in two levels along the main slope gliding down from the Mall – the vast expanse of open space right in the middle of Darjeeling, surrounded by restaurants, antique shops, bakeries, and cafes.

The school ground was a luxurious stretch of green on the first level that housed the main assembly hall and classrooms above. Around forty paved steps led to the second level below, which housed more classrooms. On its right was the palace of the *Maharaja of Bardhhaman*, a pristine white building crowned tastefully with elaborate striking blue domes. The children chuckled in delight, struggling to catch a glimpse of the numerous luxury Austins and Buicks that bedecked the acreage. Rarely could one see such an extravagant collection of automobiles in the first decade after India's independence.

Once the bells clamored for the final time during the day, one couldn't help missing the turbulent rush of navy blue and white encompassing both levels of the school campus, vaguely resembling a massive army of worker ants scrambling over a sumptuous slice of *gur*[3] all albeit curiously dressed.

Tubul walked out with a newly acquired gang, Jolly

and Bulu-Bomphat being the only ones from the old group. It was a foggy afternoon in winter.

They crossed the road in front to buy *churpis* from the local store. *Churpi* a local candy made of buffalo milk, hard and tasteless initially but melted subsequently to leave a distinct taste of mildly sweet, desiccated milk in one's mouth was a local substitute for the expensive milk caramel candies from Britain which were only reserved for special occasions.

And there was the much-extolled *aloo dum* aka spicy curried potatoes at Mangalda's shack around the corner. Khokon, his elder brother often favored them over the ones Ma made at home, making it even more coveted. Tubul counted his meager allowances and decided against it. Little did he notice a small white and caramel beast, akin almost to a blob of white sugar cotton candy, tugging at the hem of his perfectly ironed navy-blue trousers. It was Gemmy, Tubul's pet dog all of three, a hill breed endowed with an immensely woolly countenance, not that the information reckoned up sufficient mileage to the situation. He was, in fact, for qualification Tubul's best friend and had seen him conspicuously through thick and thin.

Jalapahar, the hilly stretch of Darjeeling dense with pines and heavy hill moss for most of the year, was frequented primarily during Saraswati Puja. Tubul, his brothers, and their friends frequented the place in search of cherished conquests in the form of triangular moss-laden stones which could be positioned as miniature hills when placed in the backdrop of the goddess of learning, *Saraswati* in white. Pine leaves, cones, and supplemental sheaths of moss carved out skillfully with tiny shards of tin would add the final flavor to the ambience.

Two sojourns into the terrains of *Jalapahar* would

warrant sufficient resources to last one festival at Tubul's place. However, nothing short of leeches that became succulent on your skin within minutes of each other and would have to be pulled out using generous amounts of salt was enough to deter the tiny resolute battalion.

They had it all – Tin shards, pockets full of salt to ward off leeches, pieces of cloth to tie in the treasures, and even small bamboo sticks to maneuver the bushes, undergrowth, and other minor obstacles. Moreover, everyone had an assignment. The younger ones generally fetched fallen pinecones and twigs of pine, whereas the older ones artfully carved out layers of moss and selected stones for the big day.

Tubul had wandered off searching for dismembered pinecones on one such expedition a year ago. His search had led him to a remote slope of *Jalapahar* where he had managed to collect several cones in varying hues of decay, undoubtedly beautiful. Having spent close to an hour collecting these, he had completely lost track of time and location. The children's battalion had clearly left by then and the sun casting a deep orange hue on the purple horizon, seemed to stare back defiantly as Tubul called out helplessly to his friends. There was one call, though, that answered him. Trailing almost several yards behind was Gemmy, sniffing his way past the mangle of fern and undergrowth steadily moving in his direction in valiant odds against the dubious circumstances. It was the last ray of hope from the defiant sinking sun that led Tubul all the way home - his close compatriot snuffing, huffing, panting, guiding, and stopping short only to turn behind and keep tabs on his philandering master, reprimanding him often with a short bark or two. To Gemmy, since that day, Tubul was indeed indebted.

Every sound seemed to have intensified by a thousand decibels. The voices of his friends, his mother and father, his brothers yelling, the hollering earth as it shook and gyrated with a life of its own, tearing the undulating road to Chachan Mansion into narrow slivers and then widening into gaping craters, water gushing from the yawning cavities.

Valiant cries from women and elders blowing conch shells struck terror as they waited to embrace all but the death knell – the biggest earthquake in Darjeeling.

Tubul's family spilled out on the streets like everyone else. A humongous pile of earth in the shape of the undulating Mali's garden wobbled like a jellybean before flattening itself in the process, engulfing half a dozen homes right in front of their eyes.

Gemmy, who had rushed out when the quake began, came barking in from inside the house. The vibrations gradually reduced in intensity, and there was soon but a mild tremor that shook the ground on which one stood. Gemmy brought Tubul in tow. Tubul's face and hands were caked in earth and tears ran loose. Dark brown ringlets seeped in sweat clung to his small forehead as he wept.

"Hold my hand and stop crying!" Tubul's father roared amidst the din.

Tubul's father was a heavy sturdy man, the Deputy Inspector General of Darjeeling, a very respected senior police official. He was standing there in his pajamas with his sons and wife as the world around him had rapidly changed dimensions within a matter of minutes. There was the ring of death, injury and despair in the air, the loud shriek of conch shells continuing, heightening the sheer horror of the circumstances. Pipes burst open as roads gaped wide from the quake. No one had known it was coming.

In a few days, the tremors and the aftershocks started fading away. Chachan Mansion had stood the test. Many houses in the area had surprisingly survived the quake, but there was a lot of destruction. Tubul was too young to understand the scale, but he could tell it was massive. Gemmy nuzzled up to him, whimpering, and they hugged each other as they awaited further instructions from the adults.

Over the next few weeks, Chachan Mansion became a shelter for many families that became homeless because of the quake. Tubul's father, a very generous and well-respected man in town, had pooled all his resources to help the people of Darjeeling. Over a hundred people ate meals daily for a few weeks at their home. The house was in utter disarray. Government help was slowly trickling in, but landslides on roads and quake damage did not make things any easier. There was hardly any drinking water left in Darjeeling, so people were going to the Seven Sisters waterfall in trucks. On one such trip, Tubul and Gemmy accompanied their father and his deputies the *havildars*, bring water barrels loaded in trucks until help arrived.

On the way back, Tubul's father stopped in the foggy town of Ghoom. He wanted to drop Gemmy off at his friend's house for a couple of months. Darjeeling was in bad shape and Gemmy needed to get more attention at home with the number of people living and sheltering there all the time.

Tubul did not know this was going to happen. His heart broke when they dropped Gemmy over at Jagabandu Babu's house. He was convinced that he alone could best look after Gemmy, the long walks they would go on every day and his timely meals of meat, rice, and milk. No one else could do a better job, especially not a stranger but it was hard to have an opinion when your parents decided on something during those days. Tubul cried inconsolably all the way home.

The next few weeks were spent in agony. Tubul's grief on losing his pet to somebody he barely knew in a distant town and the sheer destruction around seemed to overwhelm Chachan Mansion and their family.

On the outside however, slowly, and steadily things started getting back to normal. The roads were being repaired, and water supply was restored. Homes were getting rebuilt; shelters were in place and people slowly started trickling back to their regular lives. Tubul tried to broach the topic of getting Gemmy back, but that was the last thing on his father's list of priorities. Instead, he was responsible for restoring law and order back in the town as the situation slowly improved. There was a lot to be done and they were themselves a big family with five children to look after.

One day Tubul's aunt, who lived nearby, came to visit, and left the house door open. She had come to visit her nephews and was leaving when she saw something tugging at her saree.

'*Aay re aay re dekhbi* aay'[4] she screamed, startled from the event that was unfolding. Tubul was near the door and jumped when he heard his aunt screaming. There he was, standing, profusely panting, those puppy eyes overwhelmed with love and relief. It was Gemmy. Tubul could not hold back his tears - he squealed, leaped joyfully, and gave his pet the biggest hug he could. He felt his heart soar as he screamed and alerted everyone in the house and the neighborhood.

They learned much later that Gemmy had fled Jagabandu Babu's house just a couple of days after he was left there. He spent weeks traveling from the remote town of Ghoom, trying to find their home in Darjeeling. He had finally made it back home to his loving family, and back to Tubul. The story was almost unbelievable and unheard of in the whole town. Lost pets were rarely found or perished in the harsh weather of the Himalayas. Maybe Gemmy would go on to tell Tubul through his yaps and wags, how he had achieved this impossible feat. For now, he was just back in time for the massive bowl of mutton and rice from the kitchen that Tubul got for him lovingly.

It was the best day of Tubul's life. I will tell this story to my kids one day, and so he did.

---

1 Durga Puja – a big festival of the Goddess Durga in West Bengal, India
  2 neighborhood
  3 jaggery
  4 come see who's here

Wednesday Blues

Part I

That evening she was clad in black trousers and a velvet top with an animal print pattern. That day was when she saw him first. She entered the tiny room with its odd-sized tables and rotatable stools with their bottoms broken at the most and an occasional tear in the chocolate faux leather fabric. The tears, thanks to the teenagers sitting around and having a good time 'apparently' with their geometry boxes. That age where you are neither adolescents nor complete adults and are assumed for the most to be having a good time 'all the while'. Her entry was marked with one of the guys passing a remark that was inaudible to her, or indeed it did seem, or perhaps she didn't care. She had come for a 'make-up' class, or that was what Mrs. Sen called them, their Physics tuition teacher. It's a class you make up for when you've missed it. Mrs. Sen a thorough professional, a pioneer and an alumnus of one of the 'oh so famous' schools in Calcutta.

Anoushka came and sat down at the seat in front, the one that was located at an immediate corner of the vast expanse of a blue sun-mica study table that lay before her. Surprisingly, there were fewer girls than usual that day, and the Wednesday batch was an all-boys group, and more to her surprise was a boy who sat immediately on her right. The guys do not usually come up in front, she thought, but she changed her mind as she glanced through homework pages from the previous class. He was square-jawed, tall, tanned, and handsome in a plaid green shirt and white jeans. They were all unfamiliar faces, for she had missed her scheduled class last Friday and sat burying her head in her notebook, although she did not as much need to, with the guys behind blabbering something about the latest disco in town.

A sudden familiar voice called "Hey Anoushka, have you done your homework? I bet you haven't tried them. You had exams last week, didn't you?"

"Oh!" she said, "I tried them but couldn't get very far."

She had to look past the boy to glance in her direction. It was Shaonli sitting on the other corner of the room with an extended, rather long look. She, too, had come for the class. Shaonli gave a soft sigh. "Sen won't excuse me then, she finally concluded. I did not even try them!"

Under normal circumstances, Anoushka would have spoken to anybody next to her. Still, this boy had this distinct aura about him, which in a somewhat ambiguous manner, repelled her or perhaps endeared him to her, she couldn't tell. It was five pm - start of class, and Mrs. Sen stepped in accompanied by an aroma of Liril soap and talcum powder. "I hope you people have pepped up your math this weekend cuz'

I'll test you on your numericals", she announced. "So how were your exams, Abhishek?" she asked the boy sitting beside Anoushka. "Cakewalk", he announced, with some of the boys breaking into a series of wolfish howls and jovial banter.

The test duly commenced with the class elevens arming themselves playfully with their pens and calculators. On this occasion, Anoushka could not help borrowing a calculator from the boy, for she had forgotten to bring her own. He helped her with some subject math and smiled charmingly as she tried her best with the others. Until then, he was just this regular boy sitting in the first row, and the incident attached no further meaning to her entity.

PART II

Mrs. Sen, with her thorough professionalism, was well known for her tendency to divide her students as they were promoted to class XII based on their intelligence as to the ones who would make it to the IITs – the most prestigious and most challenging colleges to get into, the others who would make their way into the less prestigious institutes and still others who would switch over to other non-science streams after the boards were over. Anoushka was an above-average student in school, and Mrs. Sen's categorizing her into the so-called 'middle' category did not please her much. She convinced Mrs. Sen to change her timings, allowing her to come for the Wednesday evening classes, which comprised the so-called 'intelligent' batch. It was a fact though, that Abhishek also came on Wednesdays, but she did not know this.

They behaved as if they hardly knew each other the first few days. They had met just once earlier, and that too, hadn't been an acquaintance of sorts. Then one of those days was her birthday; he wished her ever so smilingly and shook hands. Then, one day when he was sitting beside her and saying something to the girls sitting to her left, she soon learned that he studied in the school that was adjacent to her own. When she told him that, he smiled and said, "I know so many people from your school! How come I don't know you?"

"How do I know?" said Anoushka.

"Yeah!" he said. "I know Nita, Ronny, Asha, Disha, Priya, Siddhi", he declared almost sardonically. "They happen to be my fan club, you know? And you are the latest to join in," he smirked.

Anoushka wasn't entertained. "Fan club?", she repeated annoyingly. She at once knew that he was one of those boys who thought no end of themselves. She withdrew and stopped speaking to him for a while. "So arrogant!" she thought, "And he thinks girls will go gaga over him hearing this! Annoying!"

The following Wednesday Anoushka was having a debate competition in school where she spotted him on her school campus with some of his friends. They had come over as spectators for the event from the neighboring school. She saw him taking one of the seats in the back row. He hadn't noticed her she thought.

They had a class that evening. She arrived in a pair of beige cargos and a melon tinted cropped top. They were running short of stools that day. It was eventually decided that they would have to share. The girls would have to share their seats with the guys in front and as Anoushka adjusted into a rather uncomfortable position that lay midway between two seats she felt a whiff of warm wind behind her ear that caused her closely cropped dark hair to fly in a direction antagonistic to gravity. She shuddered for a moment. It was Abhishek on her right, smelling heavily of his cologne who had just whispered something into her right ear. There he sat sharing half his seat with hers and giving what she felt, was a wry smile. Well, she could not help noticing that their thighs touched, even so for a nanosecond and there were goose bumps on her upper arms. After all she was straight from a girls' school, and a shy one at that who had never had any male friends.

"What did you just say?" she asked.

"Me?" "Well, I was just asking if you were comfortable."

"Oh, I sure am, thanks for asking!" she answered.

"You people had this debate in school today……not much of a success, huh?" he asked.

"Oh no! No one participated this year because of the board exams; the juniors managed to pull through somehow."

He turned when one of the boys called him from behind. They were talking about the latest Bollywood flick in town. He turned again to face her. "You saw Taal", he asked.

"Nope."

"You must hate her right, Aishwarya Rai? All girls hate her because she's too beautiful", he concluded with an air that seemed to proclaim that he had preconceived and resolute notions about the opposite sex. He focused on the word hate as he said those words. She didn't know what he meant. "I don't hate her!" she replied musingly and then suddenly alert for what was coming next.

"You don't?" he asked. "Then you are not a girl," he

blazoned out, grinning simultaneously.

"Very funny!" She smiled as she shooed him off with her colossal workbook.

That day, in class, Mrs. Sen was discussing one of the upcoming festivals in Anoushka's school.

"So how are preparations for Mantra this year, Anoushka?" Mrs. Sen asked with a general air of curiosity.

"Well things are going pretty well this year ma'am. We have tons of sponsors this year. We even have Lucky Ali coming over and performing this year on the grand finale!"

"What about the boys Abhishek? Shouldn't you be helping your sister school with the festivities?" asked Mrs. Sen.

"Ma'am don't call it the sister school please..." he said suppressing a grin causing the others in class, including Anoushka, to smile at this small joke.

"Well actually Science section A is kind of boycotting the fest...I happen to be the Gandhi of my class. Since I'm not attending, nobody else is !!" he said, asserting himself.

"Well...but that makes no sense!" Mrs. Sen revolted.

"But Maaaa'am" he said, deliberately prolonging the a's "We are tired of seeing the same faces!" he pleaded grinning.

All the boys had a big laugh at his expense. Of course, it was funny, at least for the boys. Anoushka was the only one from the so-called sister school and she too found nothing witty to respond with. She did not know how to react under such circumstances. She could either stay grumpy for the rest of the class or laugh it off. She settled for the latter. It seemed to be an easier option when the entire class was laughing.

"Nobody cares how I respond," she thought as she

looked for his reaction through the corner an eye, unable to place a finger on it.

PART III

A narrow lane led to Mrs. Sen's house. Her classes generally started at 5 pm and continued till 7:30 at the latest. While Anoushka was walking down the path day, to class, having disembarked from her Red Maruti 800, she noticed steps catching up to her slowly. She was wearing a candy pink top and a blue denim skirt that stopped short, just a few inches above her knee. She looked behind her, to see, who it was. It was Abhishek in his green plaid shirt and white jeans, the same clothes she had seen him in that first day in Sen's class. "He looks awesome in this" she thought to herself.

"Hi!" she said.

"Hiyee!" he responded.

"I didn't know you had nice legs" he said suddenly.

"What?" asked Anoushka, visibly embarrassed. She wasn't exactly too good at handling such a comment. "It sounded like a compliment but it's so forward and embarrassing. What should I say next?" she thought to herself.

A smile came to her lips although she was tongue tied and least wanted it. It almost gave her away, as if silently propagating to him, all that she was thinking. They were now walking together, and he was smiling. "Well, you needn't be embarrassed, you see, you do have nice legs!" he said again as if sensing the torment within her. "Oh god…not again! Why the hell do I have nothing witty to say?" she thought to herself.

"Well, I know that and thank you" she said smiling and finally speaking out releasing her thoughts.

He smiled a knowing smile. That day after class, she asked him for his Physics and Math School test papers that he had got to class that day.

"But could you please get them back to me this week itself; we'll be getting our scores next week, so I need to have them handy, you know?" he said.

She assured him of sending them to him through Siddhi her classmate, who went in his school bus. Siddhi was one of the anorexic girls, talkative, tall and with a svelte figure who had the boys in the neighboring school going gaga making her quite popular.

Anoushka and Abhishek had started sitting almost regularly next to each other at their tuition class and one day her physics class notes went accidentally with him. He had them sent back over to her midweek through Siddhi.

"Hey there Anoushka, Abhishek had probably taken your notes by mistake last week. Here take these" said Siddhi, one day in school.

"Oh, thanks Siddhi...thanks again for taking the trouble" said Anoushka.

"Hey how long do you know Abhishek?" Siddhi asked. "I mean he talks about you a lot these days." she added with a wry smile.

"Well, I guess for a couple of months or so...since Sen's class XII Physics coaching classes began, I mean" replied Anoushka. She was glowing inside. "So, he talks about me?" she thought her tiny heart giving out a silent whoop.

The next day when Anoushka came to class she found the boys teasing him about Siddhi. Nevertheless, she smiled at him. He turned his face and almost made a grimace. She felt a pang of pain and wondered why he did it. Why was she so mad? Was it jealousy? Did she feel threatened by Siddhi?

"No way!" she reassured herself resetting her emotions.

He was unusually seated or that she felt for he had taken one of the seats at the back. "I prefer being a backbencher", he stated stridently to one of the boys next to him as if communicating to her indirectly. Class would start in about ten minutes or so and soon Roshni came in and sat beside him. She was one of the girls, who were his 'fans' as he had proclaimed prior to her on one of his rants. Anoushka didn't think Roshni was attractive, too short for him, talkative and certainly no depth she assured herself.

"Did you get your papers back?" Anoushka asked, curious to start a conversation with Abhishek.

"Which ones?" he snapped back.

"The ones that you gave me last week, I sent them over through Siddhi", she said with not even the slightest hint of impatience.

"If someone suddenly asks you in the blue what papers, what are you supposed to understand?" he shot back. He asserted himself so very majestically causing the girl beside him to break into peals of assorted giggles and laughs and heaven only knew what else. It irked Anoushka just as it would have irked anybody else. Never had anyone, let alone a boy slighted her in this manner. "He has no right to treat me this way and how dare Roshni keep laughing at me like that! How dumb can she be to spite at another for a boy. I would never do that!" she thought, the feminist in her boiling in anger.

"I'll slap you!" she retorted playfully, trying to keep

a straight face. I probably overreacted is what she thought to herself the very next instant, but it was already late. She could no longer take back her words.

"Ha Ha!!! You will?" he peeved her further stealing a glance at Roshni who was still enjoying the banter.

Mrs. Sen had just stepped in, to start the day's lessons and the discussion stopped then and there. Anoushka avoided looking at him throughout those two hours. She knew she hated him.

PART IV

Next week they had their usual classes. Anoushka had arrived in a somewhat body-hugging navy-blue top with a ribbed white -V- neck and summery white parallel pants. He came in a good five minutes later and sat by her side. He wore a grey full-sleeved jersey and smelt of what he generally did, his Denim cologne.

"Looking good!", he complimented her, as if nothing had happened. "And sign this."

"Thanks!", she put in. "But what's this?"

"It's a teacher's day card for Ma'am."

"Oh sure!", she chimed in. She put in her signature, and he signed below her. They were talking again normally that day. Halfway through class he hid her pen, and no amount of coaxing would amount to it being produced from his end. So, they had a tiny plastic ruler fight when Mrs. Sen went in for her evening tea break. It was fun brandishing their tiny make-believe swords with Anoushka thoroughly enjoying herself poking it around on his arms. This was the closest they had ever been when it came to interacting with each other. Abhishek gave up ultimately, laughing and they both left class talking animatedly together that day.

"Was he genuinely apologetic?" she thought as he walked her to her car. It hardly mattered any longer. She did not even remember that she hated him bitterly a week ago.

Classes were off next week for Durga Puja – a famous festival for the mighty *Goddess Durga* in West Bengal. Anoushka had gone to Thailand for a holiday with her family during the school break They met a week later again on a Wednesday. She had brought along photos from her trip and her slam book. Everyone was getting their slam books to tuition classes these days. After all it was their last year in school and these books captured lovely anecdotes and fun facts from their friends.

She nudged him to see the photo album, but he seemed remotely interested.

"Now, why on earth is he acting so cold?" she thought. "Okay!" she said chirping. "If you don't want to see the pictures, at least sign my slam book!"

He observed the autograph book obscurely with a look of reluctance.

"Who do you have here on the cover? If it's Sourav Ganguly, I won't sign. I don't like him."

She didn't force him. She could have blurted out "Don't sign! Who cares anyway?" But she didn't and merely glanced at him sideways. A thousand thoughts raced across her mind. "What could have possibly happened in a week's time?" she thought and obviously found no explanation. "God, please let these moments pass" she prayed. "Probably he is just moody because it's his father's death anniversary today" she reasoned, consoling herself as she tried to make up a reason in her head. She could not bear to tell him anything, but the worst was yet to come. A few minutes later he took the slam book and started going through the pages in the beginning.

"Oh, so Siddhi's signed here" he said. Having scrutinized every word Siddhi had written, with a smile plastered on his face, and checking too that he was the first boy who was signing it. It must have massaged his ego beyond imagination as Anoushka thought later. He scribbled something in a hurry and threw it carelessly back on her lap.

"Oh, I've written something, can't write more...I find all this stuff really silly, so please don't ask me again!" he loudly stated as if he had done her a huge favor. There was silence, the entire class was looking at the two of them and she was speechless. How dare he insult her this way, when a few moments ago he was savoring all that Siddhi had written? She swore never to speak to him again.

Anoushka went home depressed that day. She was hating herself for not asking the other boys in class to sign her slam book to spite Abhishek but then she didn't speak much with the others, and they would find it odd. She was pensive for the entire week. Abhishek had misbehaved, she knew, and she hadn't even been able to respond. There was a portion in her that cried for him secretly each time, she thought about him. She cried for the way he had tortured her plain and simple soul for no fault of hers, her heart bled for him when she remembered that his father had died when he was just three years old, in a road accident. Amidst all this, she was still looking for answers, but she found none. She eventually decided to call him on his home phone. He picked up the phone, and she heard his heavy baritone hello on the other end.

"I want to stand with you on the mountain, I want to bathe with you in the sea," Savage Garden was playing in the background.

"Well...umm...hi this is Anoushka. Is this Abhishek?". Her own voice was trembling she thought.

"Well…errr..Anoushka…. oh you? Hi there!"

He was his usual jovial self as they spoke for a few minutes. He told her he was practicing Calculus and how he could never concentrate on it unless he listened to Savage Garden. They discussed, among other things the India Pakistan cricket series and how he had tiffs with his mom who insisted on watching the series Swabhimaan during the match timings, also MTV Most Wanted, how Anoushka found Shenaz the VJ cute and he thought she was plain silly and all that.

"Go and tell the world that I'm crazy about Roshni! I don't care whether she has a boyfriend!" The boys just whistled, oohed and aahed but there was no stopping him and the girl in question was so animated that she could hardly bear down her excitement or so she thought. A new girl Nisha who was quite pretty, had joined class that week. Abhishek left no stones unturned in enthralling her as well over the next few weeks.

He completely ignored Anoushka in class. She kept calling him once a week on the phone over the next few weeks, often helping him with his studies or discussing topics as the final board examinations drew near.

"Why is he always so friendly over the phone but never talks in class?" she often wondered. She honestly didn't know what she herself wanted, or more so what he expected out of her. She was always scared to make the first move in class, so they never spoke in-person.

One day over the phone she ended up asking him.

"Why do I always call you and you never call me back?"

"Oh, that's because…you call me only when you need me, that's all" he answered.

"But what does that mean?" she asked.

"Oh nothing!" he answered and moved on to other things.

On February the 13th just two weeks prior to the board exams, she called him and asked him for his school pre-final suggestion papers, offering her own at the same time.

"Can you meet me this evening Abhishek? I need the papers. I'll photocopy them and return them immediately!"

"No! You can't come, also all Xerox shops are closed today. It's a Sunday" he answered.

"Ok fine, how about I take them today and return them to you tomorrow?" she asked.

"No, I have to meet my Chemistry teacher today. You can't come today, or any other day for that matter! Do you understand that?" he snapped.

In a moment, her world came crashing down. Was this the boy she cared so much for? Was this the boy for whom she secretly cried each morning at four am when she woke up to study? Was this the boy she loved?

"Ok" she said. "Bye" her tears were choking her. She heard the line go dead on the other end before she burst into tears.

She never could read into his behavior, and after that phone call, she didn't want to either; her exams were a priority then. Anoushka topped the girls' school that year. She heard Abhishek too had topped the boys' school. She had surpassed him by a tiny margin of twelve points- in her heart that felt like a win.

Later that year after the board exams were over, she

had gone to a university campus for the BITS Mesra Engineering Entrance Exams where she caught a glimpse of him. She noticed him looking at her from a distance as she walked with some friends. But they scarcely recognized each other now. They both went their own ways, then and forever.

Masterpiece

It was Nina's thirteenth birthday, and her parents had planned a trip to Niagara Falls. She had been waiting to see this natural wonder for a good time now.

It is surprising how Indians staying in India or even in the US consider visiting Niagara as almost "the pilgrimage". It is a must-see on the agenda if you happen to be in the US for a short visit or longer and can afford it. Not that it takes a tremendous amount of money considering it is easily accessible with the various Asian Bus tour companies arranging short trips for a reasonable price. It is convenient even if one drives down from Buffalo or the northeastern states. Nina's parents could never afford the trip earlier or probably never considered the prospect – they were never much for travel or vacations. They would have reasonably considered preserving the special visit for an exclusive occasion, like her thirteenth birthday.

Nina, a lanky teenager – dark doe eyes and hair, glorious copper skin, was a quiet youngster at school. She was already in her second year in middle school and was experiencing new things as everyone did, on the eve of her adolescence. There were boys, of course, that were a sudden topic of interest in middle school. With it came the necessary baggage of who had a boyfriend and who did not and how "uncool" that was. That wasn't the only problem. For some reason, a group of youngsters in her 7th-grade class had ganged up against her and started making caricatures at her expense. She could not put her finger on the exact reason. Still, it had something to do with the undivided attention she gave Mrs. Abraham, their algebra teacher, an aged lady who had Parkinson's and made her best attempts to teach a class of unruly teenagers, topics on algebra. Nina always felt terrible for the poor lady and was probably the only one in class who saw or even cared as the teacher's eyes welled with tears at almost every lesson. Nina saw her struggle daily with a piece of chalk or her markers as her trembling hands wrote equations on the board to constant booing from the backbenchers. Each time she turned to explain, the class turned increasingly heedless and noisy, the commotion making her speech almost unfathomable. Mrs. Abraham's feeble voice did little to help as Nina struggled to hear her, even sitting in the front seat. The thing Nina did know was how knowledgeable Mrs. Abraham was and how hard she tried to get her lesson across. Nina gave her undivided attention and made sure not to miss a single lecture. Maybe this brought her haters, she didn't know. Or perhaps it didn't, she couldn't tell. Of one thing she was certain, she would never give Mrs. Abraham a hard time like the others.

Nina had other friends at the public school she went to in Baltimore. Amongst her friends were a Russian girl named Lyuda, an Irish girl named Patricia, and an Indian girl named Neha. Their parents were mainly all immigrants, too, here in the US for business or jobs. Nevertheless, a common thread bound them all as families of first-generation immigrants.

Unfortunately, soon it dawned on Nina that the section of the class that ridiculed Mrs. Abraham had gotten together to bully and bother her too. They started calling her "MP" sometimes, a derived nickname that had no connection to her real name Nina Shah. When one from the group called her MP, another would wink and yet another would burst off into giggles or both. MP was the short form for Masterpiece that she had somehow come to know. Someone in class had drawn a funny older caricature of Nina on paper resembling Mrs. Abraham, which they nicknamed duly thereafter. It was a nightmare that grew worse daily, and Nina assumed she was a joke with the boys as well.

Not that it mattered since she had her piece of consolation in the group of close-knit friends and her good grades at the end of each term. No one could take that away from her. Then again, it did matter in some ways. Ways in which Nina did not want to think of much, but whenever she did, it always made her cry. What had she done wrong? Was it so bad to be nice to an ailing senior teacher? And why Masterpiece – what was so wrong with her looks that they would make a caricature out of anyway?

She still wished to get away, and what better way than the Niagara trip during summer break. Nina's father worked at a pharmacy store in downtown Baltimore. She and her mother always walked down to the store on Fridays when he got off early, and they would walk down to the Inner Harbor. On other days, they would mostly be at home. Nina would usually return from school by three and finish her homework late afternoon before going out for her extra classes or hanging out with her friends. She would help her mother in the evenings making rotis for some Indian families that lived in the area. Some of them were immigrant Indian software professionals who had very little time and would pick up the rotis on their way back from work; others merely avoided the trouble of rolling out Indian flatbreads at home, especially when they were available so cheap and fresh. After all, who wouldn't love the taste of home so far away in a foreign land? Though not significant, the orders were genuinely regular and earned her mother a small but steady income.

The Inner Harbor was ever so lively and especially on Fridays. People of all colors, shapes, and sizes, of various religions and ethnicities, walked past. Their favorite bench was near the Children's fountain, where you could see the little ones shuffling about in the chaos, stepping between the gushes of the sparkling squirts of water, or skipping on the holes in the ground to stop the flow of water. Nina loved this place, and whenever she saw the tiny ones scurrying about, she longed to go back to those days when she had nothing in the world to worry about. When she didn't have to brood over people calling her "MP"! She would prefer to be a grown-up, have a decent job, and not care for the world. Of course, she didn't know what other problems grown-ups had, but there couldn't be many, could there? It all seemed so simple and sorted to be a grown-up.

And then, there was the harbor with strings of boats and cruises leaving or docking by day or night. Sometimes even massive foreign warships docked at the port for some military exercise or the other, and they let you go inside to look for free and meet the handsome crew in sailor uniforms.

Friday was also Mac D Day. Nina and her parents always picked up dinner on the way back to the train station. Today was one of those days, and they were leaving for Niagara the next morning. It seemed too good to be true and not just for Nina alone.

The bus was leaving at nine in the morning from the travel plaza. Nina slumped into her seat with her backpack beside her, engrossed in her latest Austen novel - Sense and Sensibility. Fortunately, or unfortunately, the Austen bug had bitten her, and the effect would likely remain for a good few years to come. Her parents sat behind her.

Oh, how she loved and adored Jane Austen. Each work seemed more mesmerizing than the one before. She visualized each book with enhanced interest and vividly imagined living in medieval England as she devoured the pages.

As soon as the bus was about to leave a family of four scurried in. Nina had barely noticed until she saw someone gesturing if he could use the seat next to her on which her backpack presently sat. She looked up and saw a confused-looking young boy, blue-eyed and reddish-blond hair, and a lightly freckled nose not much older than her. She moved her bag away and motioned for him to sit down.

"Hey, I am Jesse!" he said, struggling off his huge rucksack and shoving it under his seat. Nice to meet you!

"Hello, I am Nina...nice to meet you too. So, you're not American? " asked Nina, judging by the accent, and "Only answer if you think I am not intruding."

"Oh, I don't mind. I am English and just here for the summer".

"Cool, how long is your break? "

"Actually, I am taking a year off before high school. Just preparing for the big thing, you know!" the boy added with a lopsided grin.

"So, is it common to take a break at school...never heard of such a thing!"

"Oh yes, you take breaks all the time. Once after middle school and then after high school, right before college. Of course, most people don't go in for both breaks, but sometimes you need time to figure out what to do with life. Don't you ever feel like you need more time to think and figure out what you really want to do?"

"Well, not really.... oh well, sometimes maybe. But thinking is a waste of time. I would much rather act. And in the US, you really don't have the luxury or the time to think. There will be others burgeoning ahead if you stop to philosophize!"

"Hey, so I never meant philosophize! The break gives you time to think and decide on a direction for your life. Philosophizing is out of the question here or maybe a tiny part of it. It's more about strategizing. Anyway, forget that. Have you ever been to London?"

London! I have scarcely been outside the neighborhood, Nina thought despondently. "No, not really. My parents don't move about that much. I have always been intrigued by London, though. People say New York has bits and pieces of it, like the Broadway, but I am sure there can never be another city like London with all its history and bookstores, aah!" said Nina.

"Bang on! I have my own reasons for hating it, though."

"So, you stay in London?"

"We moved recently to Greenwood on the district line, and I abhor it. We lived in Ipswich earlier. It was an hour and a half from London by train. Quiet little town, not far from the ocean. There's a rocky beach nearby where everyone hangs out, and you have country fairs occasionally. I had friends and I loved the place. Felt like home."

"It's tough adjusting to a new place." Nina commented.

"Hmm, I guess so. And you stay in downtown Balti-more?" he asked.

"Yes, well, not exactly but nearby. How long have you been here?" she inquired.

"Well, it's been just a couple of weeks. We are at our aunt's place at Federal Hill. "There they are!" he said beckoning in their direction. "There's my cousin out there in the blue jacket and my uncle and aunt on the left. Do you know where Federal Hill is?"

"Sure do. It's right across Inner Harbor. Nice neigh-borhood! Do they stay in the pier condominiums? The ones right on the harbor?"

"Well, no, but theirs is a nice place too."

"So, how do you like the people here?" Nina turned to ask.

"I think American kids are a little upfront and maybe a touch too loud, well so far that's the impres-sion I have. We Brits always have a roundabout way of saying or doing things. Honestly, I really haven't inter-acted that much apart from my cousin brother there who's a saint. What's your impression?"

"Ah well, now that's debatable. I am American because I was born here. My parents are Indian and came here several years ago following the great Amer-ican dream. I have made some good friends here too. I like this country for sure. Sometimes you indeed feel how different it would have been growing up in India. But realistically, I could never really make out, having been here all this while. We could never afford too many trips back to India, you know!"

"Ok, so change of subject. Which book are you reading...hmm Sense and Sensibility, Jane Austen? So are you heavily into classics and love stories?"

"Well, I think I am falling in love with Jane Austen. I am yet to see the movies or the BBC and PBS adaptations, but I've heard those are great too". Do they air it on British TV?"

"Oh yeah, they air it all the time. They are well made for sure. You almost think you are in their century reliving those novels"

"Wow! I've been meaning to check for DVDs soon at the Pratt Library!" mused Nina.

"So, which grade are you in?" enquired Jesse.

"Eighth, one more year until high school. Tough life ahead."

"Tough? You should be looking forward to it? I thought all girls did! The prom and makeup and stuff, you know?"

"Well, in some ways, I do. At least, it means I am growing up. Growing up to be independent, attend college, and have a decent job afterwards. The fact is I already hate middle school, so high school is just going to get worse!"

"Is something the matter? You can share if you like?"

"Well, it's a long story. You wouldn't care to hear. It might even sound silly!"

"No, but I really want to help. Only if you feel like sharing it, that is..." Jesse trailed off.

"With me, your secret is safe. I am just here for a bit!" he said with a friendly, reassuring smirk.

Nina felt a strange sense of intimacy. It wasn't a crush or anything. Perhaps it was good sometimes to confide to a perfect stranger. You avoided exposing your weaknesses to the people around you that way. What if he thought her to be a complete fool? Or an awkward geek? Maybe she was overthinking. How did it even matter if she told this boy?

She knew her parents would never understand why she was so depressed after school these days. Even if they did, she was sure they wouldn't have a solution. It's almost incredible how young teens underestimate their parent's guidance, but it comes with the growing autonomy within, and incredibly hard to let go. Her parents would probably second-guess it was academics wearing her out for all she knew and sign her up for more extra-curricular classes.

They did not know what to make out of her sudden mood swings or intermittent bouts of silence. Her mother had hardly been to school, and little under-stood her academic progress to determine if something was going wrong. Moreover, she would be busy with her housework and roti-making business all day. Her father worked late nights at the 24-hour pharmacy, and Nina would almost always be asleep by the time he returned.

She spoke her mind. Of the travesty that she was exposed to at school. How she felt her confidence hit at an all-time low? What to do about the nickname they gave her? How much time she spent worrying about what others thought of her.

"You mean what the boys think of you," remarked Jesse with a mischievous smile.

"Oh c'mon, I should have never told you, the boys are not involved yet, but the girls give me the hardest time, aargh!"

"Hey, I was kidding. I hear you. It's usually the same sex that's brutal when it comes to bullying."

She spoke of Mrs. Abraham the elderly teacher with early Parkinson's and how she secretly cried in class sometimes, when the class bullies hurled insults at her. Of Nina trying to salvage the situation, assisting the teacher with her lectures. How Nina herself wept often, when she thought about how rude the perpetrators were, with the ailing teacher, and then to her consequently.

"There, I said it all," she said, looking at Jesse questioningly.

"Hmmm..." he replied and looked away.

Her heart sank. Why on earth did she confide to this strange boy from an unknown country she had barely known for a few minutes?

He was still quiet. Tears were forming in her eyes, and she didn't know how to control them.

"I feel sleepy," she managed to eke out and laying the book across her chest, closed her eyes. A few tears trickled down and moistened the pages. Her heart felt lighter as she took a few deep painful breaths. She struggled to overcome her melancholy, but the moving bus soon put her to sleep.

They had been traveling for nearly three hours and the bus halted at a rest area. Everyone got out, including Nina. Her mother had packed them some food for the journey. Jesse had already got off by the time she woke up. She saw him in the distance sipping on a Coke while she ate lunch with her family. He seemed oblivious to her existence.

Soon, the bus was ready to leave. Nina asked her father if he would switch places with her and went and sat next to her mother. She fell asleep again for the next several hours. She slept through the next bio break and woke up once, simply to drink water. Indeed, sleeping in a moving vehicle was the best medicine in the world, and it had come to her rescue.

When they arrived at the Niagara Falls, it was late in the evening. Everyone checked into the hotel which the tour company had arranged. Dinner was served in the hall, and everyone retired quickly after the tiresome journey. The next day would be hectic. Nina didn't remember seeing Jesse get off the bus nor did she see him afterwards when they were checking in at the hotel.

"It's all for good", she thought.

The following day, everyone was up early. People disbanded in small groups after breakfast. Nina's family had another Indian and a Korean family for company.

Their hotel overlooked the Niagara state park, a massive, ornate garden surrounding the falls. As they slowly approached the American side of the falls, dazzling in the morning sunlight, white mist rising sky high, it enthralled one and all. It was a breathtaking sight. Standing on the rails several feet above, one could almost feel the mist in one's breath. Nina was taken in by the view, as was everyone else.

"There, that's the Bridal Veil Falls," someone remarked.

True, the narrow stream of gushing white water looked precisely like a pristine milky bridal veil. It was a much narrower stream that diverted from the central American falls but was breathtaking, nonetheless. They walked over to Goat Island, the piece of land that separated the American and Canadian side of the falls to take the "Cave of the Winds" tour that took you on a stairway right under the bridal veil falls. What better way to experience Niagara than to have the water gushing down all over you?

Soon they came across a group of bridesmaids in flowy lemon-yellow dresses, hair bedecked in white roses. Somebody was having a grand wedding against the backdrop of the falls. Along came a horse carriage and the bride in pristine white, the groom in a tuxedo, exchanging vows in the park. What a breathtaking setting to have a wedding!

A little later, Nina was on Hurricane Deck, the highest point on the stairs that led right under the Bridal Veil Falls. Water was gushing down her back, at huge force. Nina almost felt overcome, by the immense power of the falling water. Almost everyone, held on tight to the slippery rails, and genuinely enjoyed the experience. Nina had some other kids from her bus group for company on the Hurricane deck. Her mother did not dare to go higher up because it got riskier with the slippery rails. Only her father joined her for that part of the tour, and she ended up loving every minute of it.

Next was the Maid of the Mist, a boat tour that took you to the Horseshoe Bend or the Canada side of the falls. After a long haul in the queue, they finally boarded the much-awaited vessel that steered several hundred people to the Canada side. What they saw was beyond imagination. It was a complete horseshoe, the massive stream of water that cascaded on all sides glistened, like a billion diamonds in the brilliant sunlight. A glittering rainbow emanated from the mist and overwhelmed them all.

As the mist caressed her face, Nina felt she was in a dream. She had never imagined a more delightful birthday. She could have never envisioned that a sight like this existed on earth and that she was there to see it. She thanked God and her parents, who she knew, toiled hard each day to make her wishes come true in every way they could. It was evening by the time they had rested at the hotel and returned to watch the night lighting display at the Niagara Falls. "Still no sign of Jesse!" she thought.

Nina walked ahead. She was excited as she took big steps across the state park. Her parents were close behind. The stream of people that had thinned towards late afternoon had started pouring in again. As she approached the Watch Tower, she felt a tap on her shoulder. It was Jesse.

"Hey..." she said.

"Hey, where have you been?" he asked.

"Didn't see you from when I slept off in the bus...so..." she trailed off.

"Well, you really didn't see me or didn't want to see me?"

"Hardly matters, does it? We'll all be gone tomorrow!" Nina said.

"Well listen here, I have something to tell you..." His face was serious.

"What is it? Does it have something to do with how silly my problems are at school and how uncool you think I am?" Nina blurted out.

"Well silly no, problems yes. And no, I don't think it's uncool."

"So, what then?"

"Do you know why I am taking this sudden break after middle school?"

"Well, I think you said they did it all the time, in England."

"Well, they do. But it's rare nowadays with all the competition. Only the Royalty have such luxury..."

"So, you related to the Duchess of Devonshire or something?" chirped Nina.

"Aha...wish I was. Well, not quite. Just this other

day, I was this quiet little boy that went to a lovely little school in Ipswich. My teachers loved me, and so did my friends. And then, well, sometime during summer, hell broke loose. My parents separated, and I came to London with my mom and enrolled in a new school.

Life changed after that. I was not too fond of school any longer. I could never tell my mother. She was always so depressed with the divorce thing, you know. She would be bleary-eyed and depressed when I woke up and often cried herself to sleep at night. I did not want to add to her troubles, but then again, I had no friends in London to confide in.

Two months later, during hockey practice. Bill...oh yes, it was Bill alright. Bill and his friends were the school bullies. They took me down on the pretext of a prep session by the coach before the finals and beat me to shreds. The following day, I was found with a fractured jawbone and a broken leg, lying near the school gutter, and almost dying of hypothermia. My mother was in pieces; that last blow to my safety was strong enough to destroy her.

Bill and his friends got suspended for a bit, but I knew others hated me for unknown reasons or possibly from influence. Probably they hit me, not wanting me to attend the inter-school hockey finals that were set to happen the next day. Their hatred was so deep and unfounded. I would never go back to that wretched school if I had to ever come out of that trauma. So, when I recovered, my mother sent me to America to be with my aunt's family for the break. She knew I would need time to figure things out and make my own choices."

Nina heard him loud and clear. She had listened to every word he said.

"So, you see...why I went silent when you told me

your story? I am sorry if you thought otherwise. It is perfectly natural to assume, but the world is not all that bad.

I used to think the way you did, but I don't think I do anymore, especially after hearing your story. It's tough to know that there are others like me in distress who are clueless about what to do and don't know how to get help.

And you know what? Your teacher, Mrs. Abraham, has blessed you for the respect you gave her, unlike your class bullies. You may not see those blessings bear fruit right now you know, but you will one day. So, there you go - that is my story. Feel any better?"

Nina was too shocked to react. They were on the Watch Tower now, and the lights display had just started. It was a startling sight, with all the colorful lights playing on the gigantic streams of water. It went on for about an hour. Photographs were being clicked all over, and thousands of flashlights went off every second. It made the whole show more magnanimous. When the show was over, she turned to Jesse.

"I am sorry for the way I thought about you. I really am!" she said apologetically.

"Hey, Nina no bother. It's natural. One more word of advice...No one ever kicks a dead dog. Always remember that there is something superior or powerful in you that they hate. All they want to do is break your confidence. You probably know what the reason is already. I know for me it was the game that I played so much better than them, and me being a total newcomer, they just couldn't handle it. Also, it is always better to confide in someone - maybe a friend, a sibling, a teacher, always your parents. I made that mistake. I never confided in anyone and ended up almost dying.

You can be rest assured that there will always be someone to support you, because you are in the right."

"Hmm...I know. Thanks for the advice. I cannot tell you how much better I feel!" Nina said, heaving a sigh of relief.

"I can tell that we both feel lighter for sure" Jesse smiled back.

Nina got together with her parents at the Watch Tower and returned to the hotel. She bade Jesse goodbye and said she would meet him on the bus the following morning. Morning came, and everyone got ready for the bus to leave for Baltimore.

Again, there was no sign of Jesse or his family. A final count was made at the hotel for the remaining guests, and the bus left. Nina overheard some people taking the next hop tour to Boston and got back to her "Sense and Sensibility" that she had abandoned the day before.

The school reopened after the summer. Nina knew what she had to do. She confided in Mrs. Abraham and a few of her other teachers about her daily torture at the hands of the bullies. The group in question was identified, questioned, and ultimately given detention for a week after the investigation was completed. Now that the matter had received due attention, things soon went back to normal for Nina. She had returned to being her happy self with the miscreants at bay. The bullies had finally left her alone as they moved on to other things.

Summer gave way to fall, and the break followed soon after. On the third day of school after fall break, the girls' team gathered at the school grounds for their first middle school hockey match of the season.

"Girls, we have a young volunteer from England to

assist me with your coaching sessions this school year," announced bald Mr. Cooper.

"He is new to our school. Girls, let me introduce you to Joshua Stevens."

A tall red-haired boy grinned as the sun shone in streaks from behind the trees. Jesse smiled and gave a friendly shrug to someone he instantly knew on the middle-school girls' hockey team.

The Rose

The warm afternoon in May was slowly melting into a pleasant summer evening as I sat on the rickety steps leading down to the garden. Dida, my grandma was sitting at the porch, a couple of steps above me, knitting a purple sweater for my fourth birthday and checking on me animatedly and occasionally.

The fragrance of marigolds, raw mangoes, and bougainvillea permeated the air as I sat preparing on my miniature mortar and pestle, a heavenly fare of yellow *daal*[1] and rice with a bit of green curry thrown in. The *daal*, of course was a rather aromatic paste of yellow marigold petals, the rice – a slug of generous quantities of squashed white *bel phool*[2] and the green curry courtesy leaves from a mango sapling. The place was Damanjodi, a town hamlet close to an industrial establishment of the National Aluminum Corporation in Orissa, India. Father tells me we were there for almost a year before we shifted base to Bombay, and I was about four years of age.

Space and time hardly mattered at that age and

particularly on that warm summer evening. Days with Dida would pass off in a jiffy whenever she'd come to visit. I remember sitting on a rocking chair each after-noon as she would tell one story after another, stories from her childhood.

Whenever it rained, the afternoons would be spent outside or in the garden making paper boats, collecting caterpillars, and setting them to sail on tiny red rivulets, courtesy of the red iron–rich soil in the region. I would steer them often with a leaf or two as my arthropod Long John silvers battled the raging torrents. Then, as these boats plunged headlong into the larger streams that trickled down the hill in front the house, I would dance in complete glee, my enthusiasm almost sadistic.

The meal was ready, and I laid out careful portions on tiny plates. I had two guests that evening, Dida, and our Nepali Bahadur also our gardener and security guard - the latter being one of the gentlest people I have met. All of sixty, I remember him as a stocky little man with innumerable creases all over his pale cheeks and forehead, tiny eyes, and a constant smile on his thin lips. I once saw him uprooting a rogue banana tree in the garden, all by himself, which amplified my regard for him several manifolds.

Dida and Bahadur ate in silence initially and would always ask me to close my eyes as they did. And when they were done, I would open them again and the food was gone, and they would tell me how lovely the dal or how well cooked the rice had been that day and how the green curry reminded Dida of her own mom's cooking. Bahadur would mostly ramble – *'bahut acchi choti didi'* [3] and again say *'hanso hanso'* [4] when I beamed, listening to the same praises repeatedly every day.

As I laid down the portions that evening, my eyes rested on a tiny silhouette of a boy coming down the road that led to the other officers' quarters. He was approaching slowly, and as he came closer; I saw he had a slight limp. He was wearing a tattered vest and pair of torn shorts, and he had bright wide eyes and a broken slate in his hand. Almost instinctively, I hailed him. He hesitated at first and then waved back. Bahadur opened the gate, and he came in limping as he did, one of his legs narrower than the other. How queer, I thought! He was a few inches taller than me and had soot on his face and hands. It didn't matter to me how he looked. I had another guest for the evening, and that meant more cooking. I was utterly delighted. 'I am going to cook for you; will you give me a hand?"

He nodded.

I don't remember what we said to each other after that, but it was instead an unspoken understanding. Almost mechanically, the boy followed me as I entered the garden to arm myself with more supplies. Our trappings consisted of a few more leaves, some bougainvillea, and fallen rose petals. I even went on to unearth some tiny potatoes with his help which I had seen Baba[5] plant a fortnight back, conveniently thinking he had dodged my notice. Baba would always remember to take me along when he dug out the fully grown potatoes but never when he planted the tubers, knowing fully well that I would be only too eager to dig them up at the earliest available opportunity. Our next object of amusement was the garden hose, which we snatched and splashed at each other, taking turns, and having a whale of a time all the while.

I had long planned to construct my own little pond in the garden, but the execution kept getting postponed because Baba was never keen. So, we gnawed at the loose soil with bare hands and wetted the earth to construct an embankment. The hose was skillfully directed at the concave surface soon after. To our utter dismay, however, the water kept disappearing.

It probably seeped in, is what I can guess when I fondly think of it now but back then we were totally clueless and disappointed. Stumped as we were, I immediately called on Bahadur to our rescue. Almost immediately, he hit upon an idea and got us a small plastic tub from somewhere. This he buried in the earth, keeping just the cavity exposed and asking us to construct our embankment around it. It was a lovely pond that stayed on till the time we left Damanjodi, with Bahadur replenishing it with water each morning when he watered the plants. We constructed a bridge atop the pond that evening, a narrow piece of plywood running across and embedded artfully into the wet embankment. Days later, I would spend hours maneuvering ants and caterpillars to follow this tricky trail!

Next, we played *ekka dukka*, a game where you limp on one leg, move on hand-drawn squares in the ground, and throw pebbles to direct the next step. Hopscotch with stones to lead the way one could imagine. I pointed at his deformed leg and looked at him questioningly. He reassured me with a toothy grin that meant it didn't matter and that he could play *ekka dukka* all the same. He not only played it better but won.

Our next object of exploration was a mound of red earth just behind the garden. Following my lead, he said he would need a long stick and a matchbox to find out what was in there. Back then, I was forbidden to play with fire and chose to smuggle him the much-needed tools from the kitchen with dexterity. He lit the match and one end of the stick while he poked the other into the red hill. Within seconds there were thousands of ants darting helter-skelter; some even creeping into the cage of the monstrous rooster next door. The rooster to our complete amusement, started crowing in visible alarm and thumping its claws furiously inside the cage. Sweet revenge, I must have thought for a moment before I panicked and screamed. Finally, being able to get back at the chickens for waking me up at four in the morning every day.

Dida who arrived amidst the mayhem, was distressed, to say the least. She instructed me to come in immediately, summoning Bahadur to rescue the poor creature.

On other occasions, after such a calamity, I would have been too scared and more than willing to be safe inside. I need to cook for my friend, please Dida, I begged though, this time. Look at all the stuff we collected, pointing to our trappings in a heap.

Grandma went in, mumbling another admonishment, asking me to play in the porch. Bring him in for some snacks I made for you Piyu - he must be hungry, poor child. He probably has a disability from polio too. I think he works at the slate factory nearby; she whispered, motioning at me to bring him inside.

Barely understanding what she meant, I chose to ignore her and set off on my new culinary expedition. The flower meal was ready in minutes but my new guest, did not ask me to close my eyes. Nor did he devour the fare of petals and leaves I had so devotedly prepared, as Dida and Bahadur did every day. Instead, he tasted it with a tiny finger and gave up trying to eat it. I was furious! He stood up smiling, unfazed, and suggested we play a new game. We were in the porch now. I hated him and pushed hard against his shoulder. He fell over and toppled into the garden. He did not cry, although his leg was badly bruised.

Slowly trying to hold himself up against his challenged foot, he managed to limp toward me. I let out a faint shriek for the first time and burst into tears. I remember distinctly that he stopped short and moved away limping on his better foot and in a few moments was back. In his hand, he held a pristine white rose he had plucked from the garden. It was the only consolation he could offer. I stopped crying and stared at him unmoved. He turned and walked away, lunging awkwardly on his injured foot.

A cool wind caressed the leaves in the bamboo forest behind our garden and gradually let out a faint murmur alongside the chirping crickets. I was still angry with the boy and went inside. When I recounted my tale to Dida in tears, she knew only too well that the reason for my disappointment was unfounded. We came out and tried to call him back. Alas, it was all too late, for he was by then a mere speck on the dusty road against the deep orange sky.

Sometimes it takes longer to fathom what happens. I wondered many years later how hungry and frail that little boy must have been. How difficult his circumstances were and yet how beautiful his mind had been. I have hated myself for being so cruel in that moment.

Each evening in Damanjodi thence, when I sat playing with grandma in the garden, I prayed that I would see him again, but that day never came.

---

1 – Indian lentil soup

2- Indian jasmine flower

3- well done little sister

4- smile smile

5- Bengali word for father

Sundari's Family

'**B**uchu eidike esho' [1] and the ground beneath him seemed to shake and so did the walls shudder a tiny bit in little Buchu's imaginary world.

The saucer of milk from the fright of the bearer gyrated wildly - overflowing its contents flat on the red polished cement floor. 'Are you feeding them again? Didn't I tell you not to?'

The summon came from none other than Buchu's father. Yes, Buchu was at it again. He was putting a saucer of milk out for the stray cat family that had taken refuge under his Baba's study table. They were a family of four– one mama and three little kittens.

Mama cat was a pristine white with sheer stripes of golden fur. The neighborhood knew her as *"Sundari"*[2] for the lovely cat that she was. The babies were a mix of exuberant grey, white, and golden fur balls – an energetic, playful little litter and brand-new to the neighborhood. For some reason, they had comfortably housed themselves under Mr. Guha's desk.

Mr. Guha was a professor at Calcutta University, and his study desk, albeit very important, was not much used for study but more for storage. There were files, papers, and textbooks of every size, color, and assortment, and the piles grew higher and higher, with there never being a sign of any order or sanity returning to them.

In part why, the offending cat family in question, had found this corner extremely comfortable to house its litter of kittens. The only times Mr. Guha went to his desk would be to add another file or textbook to his pile or to fetch a pen from his table drawer. He never attempted to sit at his chair - long worn, with creases in the faux leather and somewhat uncomfortable when Buchu sometimes tried to sit on it. It would literally poke him all over his behind, let alone the agonies of such torment on a grown-up.

No wonder his father never chose to sit there for his work.

Mr. Guha had never been that inclined to change the chair nor clean up the huge pile of paperwork on his desk or get rid of the clutter of files under them– no one really knew why. But, on the other hand, they all knew that all the stuff on his table was essential, and no one was to touch them under any circumstances.

Everyone survived and lived their lives around the colossal desk and its substantial pile of paperwork. Cleaning happened around it, the broom was maneuvered so was the wet floor washcloth. The snack plates and wet bath towels never made their way to the study table. Nothing unimportant ever dared touch the study table in the least!

The cat family soon became a huge matter of interest for six-year-old Buchu and his little sister Duggu. They watched the kittens for hours after school, getting excited at their slightest noise or movement. Of course, it was easier done when Baba was not around to reprimand them, but fun, nevertheless. They found guilty pleasure in shoving a Marie biscuit under the table or willfully overturning Baba's cup of evening tea so the cats could soak in the milky goodness. The baby cats barely ever came out those first two weeks. They did not even open their eyes.

Their mother explained that the kittens wore most likely blind and would open their eyes only several weeks later. Regardless, they watched as the little things curled their tiny bodies around their mother Sundari and drank milk from her tucked in like small yarn balls.

Their meows and baby moans tugged at the heartstrings. The children in the neighborhood loved them too. Buchu and his sister were proud owners of the cutest kittens in the community and would often have friends over to watch the tiny animals at play. The best part was that this new exhibition overtook the fancy aquarium their friend Mamun had that Buchu, and Duggu had longed for since last summer.

When the babies were about six weeks old and started walking about the house, which meant there was cat poop almost everywhere to be seen, it was just a matter of time. Baba was annoyed that his precious study table was now a permanent cat residence and smelled of cat litter. There were traces of it all around the house, and it turned out to be quite the nuisance, oblivious to the young children who thoroughly enjoyed their exciting presence.

One morning when the children were in school, Baba, with the help of some neighbors, arranged for the cat family to be transported to Kalighat, a locality about two kilometers always and known to habit many stray cats and dogs. He felt he had enough of sharing his study space at home, and the other neighborhood would be good for the young cats to blend in. In his opinion, it was the start of summer, too, so the transition would be smooth. Good riddance, he must have thought!

When Buchu and Duggu came back from school, they were mortified. It was unbelievable how their lovable cats had suddenly left, and they had no idea how. There was still their saucer of milk and tiny bits of kitten fur where they had just been scurrying about that morning.

The siblings spent the next few days and nights grieving - refusing their milk, their meals of fish and rice, and almost everything else that made them happy, including

jilipis[3] and *kochuris*[4]. Their little friends in the neighborhood were no less affected, and every other day a mother would complain of their child crying themself to sleep, reliving the unthinkable tragedy.

Buchu and Duggu somehow made it through the remaining four weeks of school until the summer vacations. It was then that their grieving resumed all over again when they started spending extended periods at home and looking at the empty desk, which had been cleaned out. All nooks and crevices from the balcony sealed too to prevent feline re-habitation.

Even their friends continued discussing and sharing their pain. After all the new cute kittens were gone, and life was no longer much fun. They reminisced how Sundari would call for her kittens when they were missing around the house or the neighborhood. The cries of the baby kittens arose time and again in their minds and tugged at their gentle heartstrings.

Buchu and Duggu would cry silently at night, worried about being reprimanded by their father for discussing the cats. Their mother secretly hoped the cats would show up again and continued to reassure them.

One day Buchu was walking down the road with his cricket bat, his tiny frame almost the size of the bat he carried and his head maybe a tad bit bigger than the cricket ball he had. He had a Marie biscuit in his hand that he was munching as he headed off to play *para*[5] cricket. After his second bite, a big piece broke off and fell to the ground. Something furry and white moved quickly to nibble at it. It was none other than their familiar mama cat Sundari with her three bigger kittens close at her heels. The kittens overtook the mom and snapped at the fallen biscuit. Buchu was overjoyed; they were back in the neighborhood. The cats had found their way back from exile or wherever they had been all this while!

Buchu wasted no time letting the children know of this remarkable turn of events. The news spread like wildfire and soon reached the adults. Every tear that fell from their innocent eyes in the last few months, had strengthened their cause, and not even Mr. Guha, with his empowering presence, had much of a say this time around.

The neighborhood took a unanimous decision to adopt the cat family jointly. A small corner at the bottom of the stairs of the town club - that also doubled as a *dhobi's*[6] workspace was made their home for the rest of the year, including the winter months. That was enough time for the kittens to thrive and be on their own in a friendly and cozy environment.

The cats moved in comfortably, and the Entally children spent the rest of their vacation stealing treats from their homes to feed their favorite neighborhood pets.

Buchu and Duggu had their best summer vacation right there in the *para*[5] with Sundari's Family.

1 *Buchu, come home right now!*
  2 *beautiful*
  3 *deep fried sweets, Bengali word for jalebis*
  4 *savory stuffed snacks, Bengali word for kachoris*
  5 *neighborhood/street*
  6 *washerman*

Curry Corner

The sun streamed in through the window jolting her out of a reverie. The bowl of oatmeal and orange juice lay by her bedside.

"There's no strength in me to get up" she thought silently wailing, her eyes gradually welling with tears. "Why am I here, even alive to see this day?" Her insides writhed in pain as she turned to face the window.

She was shuddering even with the heat cranked up and piles of blankets - her eyes and mind drifting into strobes of darkness and light.

Neel and Raina had been married a couple of years – an arranged love marriage which is nothing, but a relationship initiated by Indian families ending in a grand Indian wedding. Things were great when they started dating – Neel was a charmer and Raina was inexperienced in love, so it worked out well for both.

There was always the unsaid pressure to get married on an agreed date by parents and so they did. They had similar careers, similar outlook in life, love for good food and travel - both in the IT industry working for a global conglomerate in the United States on their work visa. Very much in love or so they thought and together after a year apart in different continents because of their jobs – they were relieved to be together at last.

Life began looking a little mundane because they were not as mobile in Suburban USA as they were back home in their big city in Kolkata, India with an abundance of public transport and chock a block with people, food, family, friends, and restaurants just a stone's throw away.

It was the month of August and Neel had purchased their first car – a second hand black Toyota Corolla for five thousand dollars. It was a much-needed tool for survival – a decent car with some forty thousand miles and Neel having got his driver's license just in time. He had taken quite a few classes and rented cars to get hands on practice – he was tired of cabbing and carpooling with colleagues and begging people to give him a lift for groceries and work.

Neel had to drive to work while Raina took the train to work in New York City. There were days when the cold weather made her lazy to go into work and she would often miss her trains. She would end up working from home most of the time.

She realized as she stayed more days at home that their work life balance was going through a shift. More and more chores got assigned to her and remained her responsibility be it the kitchen, the dishes, or the laundry. It took a while for all this to sink in and for her to realize this was happening.

There would be compliments though – every time she tried something new in the kitchen not so many at first but when she made it a point to convey how much effort she put in. Neel by nature, was not much into compliments but he outdid himself during the courtship. They truly had a very short time to know each other because of the arranged marriage situation.

As the dynamics changed in their first year of married life - the focus of their conversations started shifting more towards the dinner she would be making, special snacks she would prepare for Neel in the evenings and further and further away from her work, her career, and her life. The compliments kept her going – she would do a little more each day and wait for Neel to come back from work and comment on how clean the kitchen looked today or what a great job she did with redoing the home decor.

She became addicted to the Food Channel watching it often when she wanted to unwind. She had started to eat more as well and ended up gaining a lot of weight. Raina still made it a point to work very hard for the Company her conglomerate had contracted her to. She had a great reputation at work doing something she was over-qualified to do and ended up winning several accolades.

One evening Neel broached the topic of them starting a restaurant, he wanted Raina to consider it because she was soon getting her US residency sponsored by her company and that would have them eligible to start a business. Raina loved the idea. One, she was an extremely passionate cook and second a connoisseur of different cuisines and good food. She had no idea on business, so she was a bit clueless on the investment front.

"It's only natural" he said that you go all in with your earnings in the US. After all its going to be your venture. Just quit your job and let's do this. I will support you with logistics, meeting people and all the leg work. You focus on the capital, the food, the menu, the crew, and location.

Raina was excited at the prospect but ventured on the side of caution. She called her parents and her brother in India. She did not have any friends in the US yet, their rental neighbors in the New Jersey town were not exactly keen on making friends and she barely had gone to work enough to make friends there either.

Having been brought up in a household of highly educated women with respectable jobs in Education and the Corporate world, she was having trouble weighing her options, but Neel was adamant. "Isn't it the most obvious choice?" he would say trying to drive the point home.

She finally relented and agreed to the idea thinking Neel probably knew best – more from the confidence in his voice than anything else. She would not quit her IT job yet but soon enough once things started rolling in the right direction.

A flurry of meetings with property agents, site visits, hiring of her restaurant crew and menu decisions ensued over the next few months. With it came the pressure of Neel's parents wanting them to start a family, have their own kids.

Raina considered her options. It was true that a business would free her of a 9 to 5 schedule and weekend IT support that she sometimes had to do. Maybe it wouldn't be such a bad idea. After all she was soon approaching her thirties and it was important to have her first kid before she turned thirty in an Indian Aunties' handbook.

Neel kept broaching the topic almost every day until she finally relented. After a few months of trying, she conceived, and the couple were more than overjoyed and soon informed everyone they knew - that they were expecting a child.

"Did we order the tables?" said Raina one morning before Neel left for work.

"Can you please take care of that? "He called over his shoulder as he left.

"But you said you were going to handle all the legwork once I finish deciding"

"Babe you are just home doing nothing, you don't even commute" said Neel as he slammed his car door and left the driveway.

Raina was stunned for a minute. Did he just say that?

She hadn't even quit her IT job and here he was already calling her lazy for what. Doing a ton of chores at home, trying to start a business, and managing a full-time job and a would-be mom?

She peered through the half-opened door and saw her Korean neighbor, the man next door carrying the laundry to the basement. She would often see him helping so much around the house whenever he returned from work and then even stop to give his wife a neck massage by the window. "So thoughtful and kind" she often wondered.

"Am I getting treated like trash?" she often debated. It seemed to be getting worse every day with Neel signing up for even lesser chores at home.

Raina spent her next few days ordering the furniture for her restaurant. She was going to call it "Curry Corner". Everything was set for opening the following weekend. Her chef and helpers were ready to join, the décor was in place, stocking of supplies was in full swing. The permanent residency cards sponsored by Raina's company had also arrived authorizing her to legitimately own the business along with Neel.

She had poured all her money into this venture.

"Am I doing the right thing by quitting my job?" she wondered at times. The idea of quitting the company that was giving her so much – made her shudder, something didn't feel right. Sometimes she would look to Neel for validation. "Of course, darling, you are following your passion. What else do you need?"

His words weren't exactly convincing, but they kept her going in some ways rather than none. Everybody around her was influenced – her family though he was a gem, his family of course were head over heels for him. No one knew him as she did.

She was sensing a growing divide within her, her being on the edge with how full her plate was coupled with Neel being nonchalant about how much effort she was already putting in.

"Curry Corner" was right at the heart of the office district in Grove Street, Jersey City that had a big population of young Indian and Asians working and living in the area. There was a huge demand for good cosmopolitan food - anyone could tell. Her menu was spectacular as she redesigned and scaled up popular Indian snacks and foods with unique Western and Asian twists. They would cater mainly to the lunch crowds and the early dinner seekers and would close everyday by 6 pm. She wanted to have some sanity left for her personal life and the baby that was coming.

She quit her IT job with a heavy heart after heavy persistence from Neel and took up the business as her primary career. There were long grueling hours in the kitchen, personally inviting new customers and arranging for events, media interviews, social media channels, publicity, it was hectic. The first few months were a hurricane.

"Curry Corner" started doing great business within the first few months of opening. That was considered remarkable in the area owing to the huge rents and running costs. The eclectic menu was hugely popular as the chefs churned out great food and they soon had a loyal office-going customer base.

It was the month of February and Raina started noticing more and more Asian customers coming in to pick up their orders wearing masks. At first, she thought it unusual. She had last seen images like this during the SARS epidemic several years ago back home in India. She wondered if SARS was back.

Soon media outlets started talking about the Coronavirus in Wuhan, China that had started spreading across the world. The US was still considered safe at the time, with China being too far away and only one city in China known to be affected.

Within a couple of weeks, things changed dramatically with large number of cases and deaths being reported in Europe. In early March, all major corporations and banks asked their employees to start working from home. The office district was slowly turning into a ghost town. Customers were only trickling in now and eventually stopped coming for days together.

Raina was losing her mind, she had just made this huge investment with all her dollar savings, she had working employees, huge stockpiles of supplies all waiting to be utilized but she was not making any money. Her heart, business and money were sinking all in tandem and she did not know what to do. At home she shared her worries with Neel but there was not much he could offer her solace on.

"It's your business – he would say. Handle it!"

This after how he convinced her of leaving everything for this venture and pouring in all her finances.

She cringed every time he said this, and they would have arguments. Sometimes bad ones, but then she herself was a peacemaker and hated fights. She started avoiding the topic altogether.

One day after she had just returned from Curry Corner and cooked up some chicken curry and rice for dinner, Neel knocked heavily at the door.

"Open up quick, I have a Production issue going on. I need to login from home" he had just returned from work. She held the door as he barged in and set up his computer on the dining table. He soon dialed into a conference call and was working away for several hours. She ate her dinner and gave him his in a plate at the table and then went to her room to rest. She was in her early second trimester and felt more tired and heavier than usual. The strain of the business and the mental load of the huge loss it was making wasn't helping much. She closed her eyes as she lay on the bed and reminisced if her IT job was easier. At least she knew what she was doing there, and she needed the steady income. She was supporting her father's expensive cancer treatment in India. She went into the kitchen to get a cup of water. Neel was there as well finishing his fourth glass of scotch.

"Why is the sink so full" he suddenly snarled at her.

Raina was aghast, this was unexpected. She was on the edge, and this was clearly too much.

"Am I your maid?" she replied, her head fuming, pupils dilated in anger. She couldn't believe it was the same man she had married. He was changing everyday into this chauvinistic entitled male monster that she had been terrified of all her life. Growing up, her father and uncles had been such gentlemen, so she had a hard time believing that this was her new reality. She had known for a while now, but it was today that it really hit her.

"Yes, you are, you lazy woman. If you cook you do the dishes, you get that?"

"How dare you disrespect me like that?" she protested. "You do realize I am pregnant and running a failing business that you said you would support me on. But of course, there is nothing and never will be. Now that I am down in the dumps, I see no empathy or even an iota of help from you. What are you, who are you, are you the man I married?"

"I am the man you married, and this is who I am, and this is what you get!"

"Also, you are capable of nothing you failure of a woman, couldn't even get yourself to work when you had the job! This business just proves how much of an incapable sore loser you are. You can't even manage your household, let alone be a mom or manage a business" said Neel, raging to take her on.

Raina was in tears now – "I can't believe you are saying this. You are talking like a complete monster! What's come over you? I am worried about my life with you with a child inside me. Something has changed horribly or is inherently wrong with the way you think. All the men I have seen in my life before were avid helpers and very respectful of women. You are truly so different, clearly not what you presented to me during our few months of courtship!"

"Yes, I grew up in Dinajpur a village, yes – c'mon blame it on that. All big city fakers from Kolkata like you will blame people like us. Deal with it Raina! You chose to marry me, and this is what you get"

"And you don't deserve me" shouted Raina crying in huge bursts now.

"Die, just die Raina, or get lost. Leave me alone. I

cannot take your complaining every day, you useless woman!"

"You do realize I have your child inside of me, right?"

"Haa, yes – I don't want it. Get rid of it now. C'mon let's get rid of it now"

He pulled out a knife from the kitchen, brandishing the steel and almost instantly stabbed it into her belly. The lights whirled around wildly in her brain as she succumbed to the intense pain and warmth in her stomach and then there was darkness, complete darkness.

The metallic hospital door made a faint creaking sound as the detective walked in.

"Ma'am we've found your husband, his body was found in the Hackensack River this morning. Looks like a case of accidental drowning or suicide. Again, we are really very sorry for the loss of your baby. No words can be enough for what happened to you, but we thank the doctors, and your sheer will that you are alive and well today, after that horrific attack by your husband. We are very thankful to Mr. Cho your neighbor, for that 911 call."

"We are going to take very good care of you Ms. Raina – we have a ton of resources for victims of domestic violence that will help you. We have contacted your parents in India, and they should be calling you any minute now. We are right here by your side for any help you need." he continued, gently patting her arm.

Raina suppressed the sudden urge to vomit, briefly recalling the horrific night as those words were spoken. The detective stood out as the one godly apparition nudging her out of the darkness clouding her mind.

The strobing in her eyes took a brief pause, as she raised a weak hand to thank the nice man.

She knew then she had a life worth living, and a valuable one, even in this alien country among so many unknown people and circumstances. Something felt vaguely nostalgic of Kolkata, her home, and her people, that still valued her for who she was.

———

Author Bio

Wednesday Blues is Ananya's first book of short stories. She completed her Engineering degree originally from Kolkata, India and currently works as a Senior Executive at a reputable Financial Company in New York. Ananya and her family have been based in New Jersey, USA for more than ten years.

The writing bug bit Ananya back in middle school when she was in her teens. Her family set the stage for her to be creative in her writing by sharing interesting experiences and encouraging her to read classics while she wrote contemporary fiction. Ananya's stories, poems and creative journalism content started getting published in school and college magazines, the Times of India, Hindustan Times, the Silhouette Film Magazine, several online blogs and won her many accolades early on.

Ananya started penning her short stories in high school but never ventured to publish them as a book. Having lost her dear father and uncle in a span of one year to cancer and COVID, she embarked on a soul-searching journey to revive her passion for writing. Over the years, Ananya's life experiences have shaped her writing - be it her grandmother who would speak of her incredible childhood in Nepal or her own experiences travelling the world for work or pleasure. As a young child, Ananya fondly recalls spending an incredible amount of time daydreaming and making stories in her head. "Haven't we all?" she says smiling.